PLAYING Dirty

BETH BOLDEN

Earl Gray Publishing LLC

www.bethbolden.com

beth@bethbolden.com

Publisher's Note: This is a work of fiction. Names, characters, places, and incidents are a product of the author's imagination. Locales and public names are sometimes used for atmospheric purposes. Any resemblance to actual people, living or dead, or to businesses, companies, events, institutions, or locales is completely coincidental.

Book Layout © 2024 Beth Bolden

Book Cover © 2021 Cate Ashwood Designs

The people in the images are models and should not be connected to the characters in the book. Any resemblance is incidental.

Ordering Information:

Quantity sales. Special discounts are available on quantity purchases by corporations, associations, and others. For details, contact Beth Bolden at the address above.

Playing Dirty/ Beth Bolden. -- 1st ed.

Chapter One

It might be the first day of Tristan Nicholson's life post-university, but instead of feeling like he was finally a professional football player now, it felt like he was right where he'd just left: back at school.

Technically, you are *back at school,* Tristan huffed inwardly as he shifted the new Louis Vuitton duffel bag he'd splurged on to look like a "real" player and not just a rookie picked in the dregs of the fifth round.

The Miami Piranhas held their preseason camp not at their own practice facility, located in the heart of the city, but further north into Florida, at South Orange, a small Division III school just outside Orlando.

Which meant instead of finally starting his NFL career by heading to the Piranhas Stadium, he'd driven his rental car to yet another campus.

Tristan pushed open the front door to the main building of the athletic complex. There was a Piranhas banner hung behind a temporary table set up in the foyer. A young-looking guy, maybe not too many years older than himself, in dark-rimmed glasses and a white polo with an embroidered Piranhas logo was standing behind it.

Tristan walked over, adjusting his bag on his shoulder again. For designer merchandise, it was hella uncomfortable, and he was already missing his old, worn duffle. But he'd wanted to make a dynamite first impression.

"Hi," Tristan said, "I'm here to check in for camp."

"Tristan Nicholson, right?" the guy said, shooting him a friendly smile. "I'm Beau. Nice to finally meet you."

"You too," Tristan said. Wondered what this Beau guy did for the Piranhas—besides being tasked to greet all the rookies who were showing up today.

"Here's your orientation packet," Beau said, passing him a thick shiny turquoise folder emblazoned with the fighting piranha logo. "We'll be having weigh-in and equipment checkout today, as well as a quick medical check."

"I'm healthy," Tristan said hurriedly. He'd had a bum ankle injury that hadn't wanted to heal from over-training for the combine, and he'd missed the optional training days earlier in the summer. He'd flown in just to have the ankle checked out by the Piranhas staff, and then flown right back out without meeting anyone. They'd sent him home with a whole playbook to memorize and firm instructions to stay off his ankle.

The Piranhas doctor had insisted he stay off of it for a full month, and it *had* healed, but now Tristan was afraid he was even more behind.

"That's great to hear, but it's just a basic check, to make sure you're good to go for the conditioning trial."

"Right," Tristan said. His agent Alec had told him about the conditioning trial, and how he'd probably pass it with flying colors, but it was impossible not to be nervous.

Especially when he'd only been working out again for a few weeks.

"And," Beau said, pulling out a list, "last thing is getting you a room number and a key. You'll be sharing with . . ."

But Beau didn't finish the sentence because the door behind them opened and then closed with a swish, and then there were heavy steps approaching.

Tristan glanced behind him, looking at the newcomer, and then *kept* looking.

He recognized him, of course.

The Piranhas hadn't drafted *that* many players, after all, and he'd dutifully followed all their social media accounts because while that was the kind of gesture that might be hollow and meaningless, to Tristan it felt like he was actually *doing* something to prove that he belonged, just as much as the next guy. He'd briefly glanced at each of the profiles, and had been able to pick out who clearly didn't run their own pages.

Wade Lewis had gotten a fraction longer examination, and Tristan wasn't stupid enough to pretend cluelessness as to why.

In person Wade Lewis was even more impressive, tall and built like a tree trunk, solid and unmovable, with muscular legs and arms exposed by the t-shirt and athletic shorts he wore.

His brownish-blond hair was pushed back, unstyled, he had a few days of golden scruff on his chiseled jaw, and his light gray eyes were confident, betraying none of the anxiety currently swirling inside Tristan.

Probably because Wade had been drafted early in the second round, and was practically a lock to make the roster, because the Piranhas desperately needed a solid tight end.

Yes, he was hot.

He also had no idea he was hot.

And, Tristan added, even though he'd long since given up lusting after all the straight football players in the various locker rooms he'd belonged to, *he's not for you.*

"Hey, Wade," Beau said, and to Tristan's surprise, they did some kind of complicated handshake thing.

Another reminder that Tristan, who was right on the fringe of not belonging anyway, had missed an important bonding opportunity because he hadn't been able to work out at rookie camp.

His fingers itched and he wanted to whip out his phone and ask Wade if he wanted to take a selfie for his Stories, or maybe a quick video, two freshly drafted rookies meeting for the first time, for the reel he wanted to put together for his first day.

"You've gotta stop trying to use social media to deflect from your insecurities," Alec had told him just last night when they'd discussed Tristan's first day.

It wasn't that Tristan didn't think Alec wasn't right.

Alec had told him, very frankly, that he'd had three strikes against him, despite his speed and skill as a wide receiver. *One,* he'd gone to a smaller Division III school. Less competition. Less shutdown defenses. *Two,* the lingering ankle injury. *Three,* Alec had added ruefully, you're more famous for your Instagram feed than you are your touchdowns.

Tristan hated that his social media, which he'd initially started as tangible proof that you could be young and attractive and gay and also a freaking good football player, had ended up becoming a strike against him.

Had he come to rely on it too much?

Maybe Alec wasn't wrong.

So his phone stayed in his pocket.

Yeah, but if you took a selfie with Wade Lewis, you'd get to touch him for just a second, and that would be jerkoff material forever.

Tristan ruthlessly pushed that thought to the side, pushed it down. Out of his mind. It was habit now. He didn't find *every* football player attractive, but he had a firm "no players" policy, which had worked out for him pretty well so far.

He wasn't going to lose his mind over the likely straight Wade Lewis.

He definitely wasn't going to compromise his chances to make the Piranhas final roster for him.

"I said, *hey*," Wade said, his voice edged with the beginning of annoyance.

And Tristan realized he'd been standing there, staring at Wade Lewis, who'd actually been talking to him, and he'd been totally spaced out.

Thinking of all the things that he wasn't supposed to be thinking about.

Shit.

"Oh, hey," Tristan said, pasting on a bright confident smile. "I'm Tristan Nicholson."

"Wade Lewis." Wade's handshake was solid, just like the rest of him. If Tristan felt a thrill somewhere he had no business feeling a thrill, he ignored it. "I've watched some of your film; you are *fast*, dude."

"Oh, thanks," Tristan said, surprised. Wade Lewis had watched *his* film?

"You got totally fucked over, *fifth* round, what was that about?" Wade's smile was completely genuine, just like the Texas twang in his voice. "But I told Beau here that you guys got a freaking steal. You're gonna just breeze by everyone in the NFL."

"Wow," Tristan said, even more shocked now—because it was *Wade Lewis* saying this to him. He knew he was fast. That wasn't news. But Wade's interest? That was unfortunately way too intriguing. "That's . . . well, thanks, that means a lot."

"I was just telling Wade that it's good you guys have some kind of mutual admiration society, because you're sharing a room," Beau spoke up.

"We're . . . we're sharing a room?" Tristan hated that he stuttered over the words. Did that expose him?

You can't be exposed. You have four million Instagram followers. Everyone on planet Earth already knows you're gay.

"Yep," Beau said. "All rookies have a roommate. And Coach Dawson didn't want to encourage too much competition by forcing you to room with a player who shares your position."

Except that Wade *was* his competition.

They both needed to be their very best at their position if they had a hope of making the team. Wade had the edge, because he was a tight end and that was a position of need for the Piranhas—and they wouldn't want to release a second-round pick—but Tristan? He was right on the edge, and he knew it.

Anxiety churned in his stomach.

"Well," Wade drawled, "that makes a whole lot of sense. I'm sure it'll be great to share with Tristan." He clapped Tristan on the shoulder, *hard*, probably because he was so . . . well, he was a lot of things.

Things that Tristan absolutely wasn't going to think about. Tristan ground his teeth together.

"Right, totally."

If he was going to share his room, he'd have much rather shared with a lineman with smelly feet and a sweet smile—a guy he wasn't going to be attracted to.

But he could do this.

Correction: he *had* to do this.

"Better get settled in," Beau said, "the weigh-in is starting in an hour."

"Oh, I'm so excited about that," Wade said, the sarcastic edge to his voice and the glint in his eye making it clear that he wasn't at all.

Which, from Tristan's perspective, was a little fucked up because while Wade was *big*, it looked like every inch of his body was muscle.

"Yeah," Tristan said weakly.

He wondered if the NFL version of the weigh-in would be anything like the MMA ones he'd watched with his ex-boyfriend in high school, where the competitors stripped down, willing themselves to make it under weight.

For a split second, he imagined what Wade might look like in only a pair of tight boxer briefs stretched tight over his undeniably muscular thighs.

And then Tristan realized that no matter what the weigh-in looked like, he was going to get a front-row seat to that incredible vision and possibly even more.

Because he and Wade were sharing a room.

Double shit.

"You ready, roomie?" Wade asked.

"Yeah, yeah, let's go find our room," Tristan said. The good news was that Alec had already warned him that he'd be busy from dawn to dark, between the weightlifting sessions, endless meetings, and two full practices each day.

Maybe he'd be too tired when he fell into bed to even care if Wade's Thor build was displayed in HD right in front of him.

"Here's your keys," Beau said, passing them across the desk. "See you two at the weigh-in."

So that was Tristan Nicholson.

Wade had looked forward to meeting the speedy wide receiver after watching his film, but the problem with watching film was that in full pads and helmet, you never got a good impression of the *man* playing the position.

Well, he had a damn good idea of the man now.

Of course he'd seen pictures of him before.

It was impossible to be in the NFL—or to have played serious college ball—and not seen Tristan Nicholson. He was everywhere, and even though Wade didn't spend much time on social media, he'd definitely seen the guy.

Pictures didn't do him any justice whatsoever.

From the second Tristan had flashed him that bright, wide, cocky smile, blue eyes flashing with confidence, Wade's pulse had been all over the fucking place.

He'd known Tristan was attractive.

He'd also known he was bisexual for awhile now, but he'd never met a guy who sent his heart rate into overdrive. He'd definitely never had it happen with another player.

He'd *never* expected that it would happen with Tristan Nicholson.

His new teammate.

His new *roommate*.

That was inconvenient . . . or, Wade thought speculatively, as he watched Tristan put his designer bag on the bed on the right side of the room, maybe he just wasn't looking at this the right way.

It wasn't that he was against exploring this part of himself; he'd just never had a chance before. And if Tristan was right there, and if Tristan happened to be interested right back . . . except that he didn't think he was, even if he *was* into guys.

Since they'd met, Tristan had been distracted and kinda all over the place, and Wade told himself he understood.

This was an important two weeks for Tristan. He'd fallen to the fifth round, and now he needed to make a big impression in camp.

Wade resolved that even if Tristan wasn't attracted to him—and who could blame him if he wasn't? He was nothing like the slender, delicately muscled, absolutely fucking gorgeous wide receiver with the designer taste and the legion of social media followers—then at least they could be friends. They could help each other through the next few weeks of hell.

"It's . . . well, I never expected that I'd be back in a place like this," Tristan said ruefully as he turned around the room. He'd taken his phone out of his pocket. He was wearing jeans and a t-shirt, but he made them look impossibly good, like he was a freaking model.

Nobody real had eyes like that—impossibly light, clear blue. Like the Caribbean Sea.

Except that Tristan was definitely all too real. And he was right in front of Wade.

"Back at school? Yeah, it's kinda weird feeling," Wade agreed. He pulled his sheets out of his bag and began to make the bed. The mattress was thin and he could already tell it wouldn't be long enough for him.

Wade resolved himself to cramped, uncomfortable sleep while they were here.

Tristan had pulled sheets out of his own bag, but when Wade glanced over, he was carelessly tucking them in, tossing a bright turquoise blanket over the top.

Wade finished tucking his own in, making sure the corners were nice and tight. If his father was here, they'd have passed inspection.

"What do you think we should wear for the weigh-in? Do you think we're going to be heading to the fitness test right after?" Tristan was staring into his bag, like it was going to share the mysteries of the universe.

Wade shrugged. He never knew what to wear, so he just wore what was comfortable. He'd already begun to pull out his own meticulously folded clothes, transferring them to the drawers on his side of the room.

"Well, I guess I'll change just in case."

Wade saw him glance towards the attached bathroom and then back to Wade.

Did he not want to change in front of him? Wade thought that was kind of odd. They'd all learned to be immune to taking their clothes off in front of strangers long ago. Maybe . . . because Tristan was gay and so freaking hot, he felt differently about it.

He politely turned his back, but not before he got a single glimpse of a slim, perfectly proportioned chest, with slim, firm muscles under tan skin, and just a smattering of dark hair leading to . . .

Wade felt his breath stutter.

It was so unfair that after all the guys he'd played with over the years, this was the only one who'd ever reminded him that while he'd never been with a man before, he was definitely, undeniably attracted to them.

But why would a guy like Tristan Nicholson ever look twice at him?

He was famous not only for being a great football player, but for being out and proud and never taking an ounce of anyone's shit.

Wade had always admired him because he'd always been honest—sometimes brutally so—about who he was and what he believed in.

"Okay," Tristan said uncertainly, like he didn't know what to say, and when Wade turned back around, he also felt more awkward about it than he'd expected.

They'd be changing around each other before practice.

Naked together in the showers.

Wade was tempted to run back to the athletic complex and tell Beau that this wasn't going to work out after all. But then Tristan tipped his head up and met his gaze with steel in his own.

Wade recognized the determination because he'd felt it too, so many times over the years.

"You don't have a problem with this, do you?" Tristan asked.

Wade wasn't stupid enough to know what he was asking. Or why.

You were stupid enough to turn around, Wade chastised himself, *and now he thinks you're going to treat him different because he's gay.*

"No," Wade said. Considered saying more. Considered saying, *"hey, by the way, I'm also bi, but I've never acted on it, and I've never really been tempted, not until you. So . . . hey, there's that."* But he didn't, because how silly did it make him look, with all his curiosity and no action, when Tristan was *all* action?

"Good," Tristan said with a sharp nod. "I wouldn't want there to be a problem."

"No problem," Wade said, feeling like he should apologize, or grovel, or *something*. "It's . . . it's *really* not a problem."

Tristan's expression softened. "Okay, I just wanted to make sure. At school, well, everyone knew, from day one, and nobody cared because we were just happy to be playing ball, but here . . ." He hesitated.

"It's different," Wade finished. "This is the big time."

"Yeah. Yeah, it is." Tristan's smile was genuine now, the most genuine that Wade had seen it so far. And he thought, *yeah, we might be able to be friends, after all.*

"I guess we'd better go deal with this weigh-in bullshit," Wade said.

He wasn't nervous about not making the weight the Piranhas had asked—but it still felt like taking a quiz, on the first day of school.

Needing to know the answers before he'd ever known the questions had always made him anxious.

"You actually worried about making weight?" Tristan had grabbed his ID card from his bag and tucked it in the pocket of his shorts.

Wade sighed. "No, not exactly. But it's . . . you gotta do everything right, you know? Even when you don't know what's right."

"Me, *yes*, you, I'd guess you've got a little more leeway," Tristan pointed out shrewdly as they headed out the door.

"Because I got drafted in the second round?" Wade wasn't sure he completely agreed with that assessment. "I guess we'll see. Their expectations might be higher."

Tristan made a noncommittal sound as they walked down the stairs and then Wade pushed the door open for them.

The walk to the athletic complex was only five minutes, which Wade knew he'd be grateful for later.

There was a group of about twelve rookies milling around the foyer when Tristan opened the door and they walked in.

"Oh, good, we're all here," Beau said. "Let's get this going."

He led them all into the locker room, where they'd set up a scale and he called each player's last name in alphabetical order.

When Beau said, "Lewis," Wade stripped off his t-shirt, and forced away that brief second of nerves. He'd told Tristan that it wouldn't be a problem, and damnit, it wasn't going to be. He wasn't going to treat him different than he treated any of his other football brothers, just because he was gay. Just because he was attracted to him.

Wade stepped on the scale and stared straight ahead as Beau checked the electronic readout.

After all, he'd done a lot tougher things, right?

"Great job, Wade," Beau said, absently patting him on the back as he stepped off the scale. "Right where we talked about."

Wrangling his shirt back on, Wade caught Tristan's glance over at him. There was amusement there—like he hadn't believed that

Wade had anything to worry about—but also support and under-standing.

It was one thing to think Tristan was attractive, because he was, there was absolutely no denying it, or that he was definitely attracted to him, but he hadn't really expected Tristan Nicholson to be so damn *nice* or so down to earth.

"Nicholson," Beau called out next.

Tristan did the exact same thing Wade had, stripping his shirt off perfunctorily, and stepping on the scale.

Wade absolutely did not enjoy seeing the flex of his back muscles.

Nope.

No way.

Beau leaned in, peering at the number. "Missed those few weeks of workouts, huh?" he asked and Wade caught a glimpse of Tristan's grimace as he pulled his shirt back on.

"More protein shakes and pasta?" Tristan muttered.

It occurred to Wade suddenly Tristan had actually been *under* weight.

It was unfair because from where he was standing, the guy was goddamn perfect.

Two more guys went—the last of the group—and then Beau was leading them through the locker room, through a maze of hallways, until they reached an open doorway.

"This," Beau said, "is the equipment room while we're here at South Orange. If you need anything, Lyanna is the person to talk to. Go ahead and check out what equipment you still need, and be fitted for your helmet, and then I'll pull you out one at a time for the quick medical clearance."

Wade saw a flash of something on Tristan's face again, and as everyone dispersed, milling around the equipment room, he tried to nonchalantly move over to him.

"Missed some time, eh?" Wade said, keeping his voice low so that they wouldn't be overheard. He'd known that Tristan was nursing some kind of injury, which was why he hadn't been at rookie camp, working out with the rest of them.

Tristan glanced up at him. His eyes were otherworldly, a shimmering blue ocean that Wade wanted to get lost in, even though it was the worst idea he'd ever had.

"Yeah," he said shortly. "Sprained an ankle a few months back, right before the combine, and it wouldn't heal."

It occurred to Wade that Tristan hadn't been at the combine either. This would be why. It might also explain why Tristan had fallen to the fifth round, when he'd personally thought he should've been taken much, much earlier.

"Because you wouldn't stay off it?" Wade asked.

"Yeah," Tristan said. "And then I *had* to, after the Piranhas drafted me. They wanted me healthy for training camp. But I lost some valuable weeks."

"You'll get back in shape," Wade said, and then realized stupidly, at the last moment how that sounded.

Tristan flashed him a smile, like he knew why Wade had total-ly stuck his foot in his mouth. Even though he couldn't possibly.

But then . . . maybe Tristan Nicholson was used to tying men into knots, effortlessly, without even meaning to.

He'd certainly done it to Wade.

"You know what I mean," Wade stuttered out. Never hating more than he did in this moment that he was *bad* at this.

Of course, what would happen if he was good at the whole flirting, being-attractive, being-irresistible kind of thing?

Absolutely fucking nothing.

"I do," Tristan said, that irrepressible charm practically ooz-ing out of him. He patted Wade on the shoulder. "But it's okay. And I appreciate the sentiment." He flashed him another grin. "Don't take it easy on me, okay?"

Friends, Wade reminded himself, they were going to be *friends*.

"Absolutely not, I swear."

"You two done flirting over here or should I come back?"

A woman's voice, authoritative and sharp, cut through the haze of Wade's crush.

Because that was what it was, right? A fucking crush.

Wade shook his head free of the sticky, gooey strands, all which wanted to entrap him and lure him into doing things that he had no business doing.

"You must be Lyanna," Tristan said smoothly, recovering his wits first. "Our lovely and capable equipment manager."

She shot him a knowing look. "Think you're charming, do you?"

Tristan just shrugged.

"Let's get you fitted for your helmet," she said, all no-nonsense. Her dark hair was pulled back in a sleek ponytail, and there was a spray of freckles across her nose. Wade had encountered her once or twice when he'd been at the optional rookie workout days, and he already knew you could be either on her side or on her shit list, and he already knew which he wanted to be on.

Which you *needed* to be on, if you had a single brain molecule in your head.

"Wade," she said, waving a hand, "you might as well come too, though I fitted you a month or so back. You decide which grill you want on the front yet?"

"No," Wade admitted as he watched Tristan examine all the helmets. "Think it might depend on the day. Sometimes if it's really bright, I think I might want the full coverage."

Lyanna nodded. "We can do that. And hey, it's Miami"—the corner of her mouth twisted up—"probably more likely you're going to want it. But I can do both."

"I thought only defensive backs trying to be intimidating as shit wore those," Tristan said, his tone teasing.

Wade was reminded that Lyanna had accused them of flirting. He tried not to flush.

"I've got light eyes, sensitive to the sun," he explained.

"Ah," Tristan said. Craned his neck and really *looked*.

Don't you dare blush, Wade ordered himself, don't you dare fucking blush right now.

"You really do," Tristan said with a smile. "Like the sky after a bad storm."

Lyanna raised one dark eyebrow. "I pulled the two styles you wore in college," Lyanna said to Tristan. "But you can try something else, if you wanted."

"This is fine," Tristan said lifting one with an open-work grill at the front and the additional concussion cushioning on the crown. Some old-school players didn't like them, because they were bulkier. But Wade believed in being safe rather than sorry. He didn't want to end up a statistic and a brain being dissected in a lab.

And it seemed Tristan didn't want to either.

He wasn't just hot. He was smart, too.

That, Wade realized, was the *real* danger.

"You feel better about it now?" Wade asked, as they lay in bed after a long day.

And, Tristan thought, the days are only going to get longer from here.

He'd just flipped the light off, said his goodnights, and fully expected that Wade would turn over on his bed, on his side of the room, and fall asleep.

But instead he'd asked that question.

"Better about?" Instead of answering, he asked another question back, even though he had a pretty good idea of what Wade wanted to know.

"You know," Wade said, waving a hand, Tristan barely able to make out the movement as his eyes adjusted to the settling darkness of the room.

"They cleared me medically, and I made it through the fitness test in one piece, passing with flying colors. And I was only half a pound underweight." Which he'd probably made up for already with the enormous grilled chicken breast and plate full of pasta he'd consumed at dinner, alongside the ubiquitous protein shake. "So yeah, I'm good."

Wade didn't respond right away.

"That wasn't what I wanted to know."

Tristan knew that too.

He'd just hoped that Wade would let him have this.

He wasn't the only "out" player in the NFL. Colin O'Connor had come out ages ago, and there'd been a number of guys after him. Spencer Evans, who'd played for the Los Angeles Stars, but now played for the Riptide. And all those other players on the Riptide: their kicker, and their quarterback, and of course, everyone knew about Chase Riley. There were a handful of others, scattered over the rest of the teams. But that didn't necessarily make it easier.

Tristan wasn't sure he even wanted it to be easy.

If something grew easy, you forgot how tough the going had been—both for himself, and for others.

"Do you mean, am I relieved you're not a homophobic asshole?"

It was also easier to come out aggressive than to wait and be victimized.

Tristan wished he'd never learned that lesson the hard way, but he had, and he'd never forgotten it.

Wade chuckled under his breath. "Uh, yeah, I guess?"

"You're not terrible," Tristan teased.

An understatement.

Wade was not only smoking hot, but he was surprisingly sweet too, under that huge frame and all those muscles. A big teddy bear. One that Tristan was definitely not going to be tempted to squeeze.

He'd watched out for him through checking out his equipment, barely leaving his side, and he'd had a feeling that Lyanna had found this particularly amusing. He'd checked in with Tristan after his medical exam, and also after the fitness clearance, skin still slicked with sweat.

Looking, Tristan tried hard not to remember, completely fucking edible.

"Well, thanks, I'd hate for you to . . . well, hate me," Wade admitted into the dark.

"I don't hate you," Tristan said.

"I . . . I respect you a lot, actually," Wade said, and there was a deep, quiet appreciation in his voice. Which shouldn't have surprised Tristan, but it did. "I've followed your Instagram posts. You've done a lot of good."

"I didn't realize you were a fan."

It was easier to tease than to internalize the praise. Tristan wasn't proud of that particular fact, but it was the truth.

"I . . . I haven't told anyone this." Wade was still stuttering a bit, but Tristan would've recognized his hesitation even without it.

"Told anyone what?"

But Tristan knew what was coming.

At least he was *afraid* he knew what was coming.

It had been easier to pretend that Wade Lewis wasn't a tree he'd like to climb, over and over again, if he thought Wade was categorically not interested.

If Wade was straight.

But unless he was mistaken, Wade was about to tell him he wasn't.

It was a dream and a nightmare, wrapped up into one complicated package.

Tristan heard Wade take a deep breath. "You're so fucking honest," he said, wryly. "How do you learn how to be that honest? I'm no good at it."

"I think you're better at it than you think," Tristan said sympathetically. Even if Wade not being straight made his life a lot harder, he wasn't going to let him know that. Wade deserved his listening and his empathy. "Believe it or not, it's never easy. Even when it looks easy."

"Well, it's not easy," Wade huffed. "Anyway, I thought I wouldn't tell you, because I was embarrassed you've been so honest for so long, and I've . . . well, not been hiding, but not been entirely honest. It just never came up, and then it did, but it didn't matter, but then it also felt wrong to not tell you, because we're . . ."

"Friends?"

"Yeah," Wade said, sounding relieved.

"You can tell me, Wade."

You can take me. You can have me any way you want me.

Not the point, Tristan reminded himself. Not even remotely close to the point. Yet also still true.

"I like girls too, you know, and well, guys too, I suppose. I've always known it, but there's never been . . ." Wade trailed off.

"Sexuality isn't a black-and-white construct," Tristan said softly. "You can be *more* attracted to women than men. You can be attracted to a person, rather than a gender, too. There are no rules."

Wade was quiet for a long time. Just when Tristan thought he'd gone to sleep, he spoke up again. "I'm bisexual," he said. The words were soft but they fell like bombs into the darkness.

"Congratulations, Wade," Tristan said. And reminded himself for the hundredth time that Wade's confession didn't mean he was attracted to *him*. It just meant that he saw a sympathetic ear in Tristan, because that was the role he'd constructed for himself over time, wasn't it?

It wasn't always what he'd wanted but he'd grown into it, one confession like Wade's at a time.

"Thanks for listening," Wade said and there was that same relief in his voice that Tristan had heard in so many over the years.

But for some reason, Wade's confession felt special. And without even meaning to, Tristan gathered it close and let the warmth and honesty of it comfort him as he fell asleep.

Chapter Two

"Who *is* that guy?" Tristan gestured with this fork. "He looks familiar but I swear I can't place him. And everyone's so deferential around him."

Wade looked up from his morning eggs, and saw that Tristan was pointing in the direction of Beau.

Beau had his dark-rimmed glasses on, and was surrounded by papers, with both a laptop and a tablet set up in front of him that he kept returning to—but no people. Nobody had sat at his table, which made sense.

"Beau?"

Tristan nodded.

Wade had worried in the wake of his late-night confession that things would be weird or awkward between him and Tristan.

That Tristan might make the logical leap and assume that Wade had told him he was bi because he was attracted to Tristan. But Tristan hadn't made any assumptions. He'd just taken his words and absorbed them and then treated him exactly as he had before.

It both frustrated Wade and also gave him a peace he hadn't ever imagined he'd find.

He was accepted, just as he was, by at least one person.

It was shocking how much of a difference that made.

"You don't know?"

Tristan shot him a look. "If I knew, I wouldn't have to ask, would I?"

"I just thought . . . well, you're so tied into the community and stuff . . ."

"The community? The football community?" Tristan's voice was wry. "Not as much as you might think. I did play ball at some very minor Division III school, which the sports media wastes no time reminding me just about every moment of my life."

"No, I mean . . . the *queer* football community."

Tristan narrowed his eyes. "Should I know Beau?"

"He's Coach Dawson's son."

Tristan's fork clattered onto his plate. "*What.*"

"Yeah, he's Beau Dawson. I thought you must have recognized him, because I know it was big news a few years ago, when he came out and everyone wondered if Coach would support him."

It had been big news only because Asa Dawson had been one of the most successful college coaches ever, and on top of that, one of the most famous *Southern* coaches, renowned for his unconventional methodologies. Nobody had known how a guy who was literally known for eating the stadium grass before a game would react to having an out and proud gay son.

But Coach had surprised everyone by being fiercely support-ive.

It was one of the reasons that Wade, even though he had never really considered coming out before, had been so relieved to be drafted by the Piranhas, even though they had been historically bad the year before.

Everyone was interested to see what Asa Dawson would do, in his first year as an NFL coach, to turn this franchise around.

But Wade was just glad to play for someone who wasn't a homophobic dick.

"Well, that explains why nobody's sitting with him," Tristan said, practically dislocating his neck to get a better look at the man. "It'd be like sitting with Coach. But yeah, now that you say it, that's why he looked familiar. I wonder why I couldn't place him."

Wade had a sudden and terrible thought that maybe *Beau* was Tristan's type, and that was why he was suddenly so interested.

"Well, he grew up," Wade said wryly. "He came out when he was seventeen. And he's what . . . twenty-four now?"

"And working for his dad," Tristan mused.

"Yeah."

"You met him at rookie camp," Tristan stated rather than asked.

"Yeah, he's a solid guy. He's helping his dad out, and told me he'd be here early, to work with the rookies. He's like a genius statistician, or something."

"Huh." Tristan still looked surprised by this.

"I thought you knew everyone there was to know," Wade teased him lightly.

Tristan shot him a look. "I did get to meet Chase Riley."

"Really?" Wade leaned forward. Suddenly very interested.

"Yeah, he gave me some pointers, though . . ." Tristan grinned. "He's built a bit more like you than me."

"He could've been a tight end, but he's shit at blocking," Wade said bluntly.

Tristan's eyes widened. "You wouldn't dare say that."

"What?" Wade shoveled eggs into his mouth. "It's true. He'd probably be the first person to admit it."

Tristan laughed. "Probably," he agreed. "He's a great guy. Totally self-deprecating, which you'd never imagine Chase Riley could be, but he *is*."

"How'd you end up meeting him?" Wade asked, and then felt really stupid. Tristan had met him because he was *Tristan Nicholson*. Division III athlete or not, fifth round or not, he was incredibly well-known and basically universally beloved.

But Tristan tilted his head and didn't seem annoyed by the question. "We share an agent," he said. "Alec Mitchell. I spent a few weeks in California, at his workout facility, and Chase was there."

"That's so cool." Wade knew he sounded like a fan—but he *was*.

"Wish I'd gotten to do more while I was there," Tristan said, and a frown crossed his handsome face. "This stupid fucking ankle."

"It's better now, though, right?" Wade asked.

He'd passed the medical exam, after all.

"Oh yeah, it is, just lost time." Tristan made another face. "I know I need to work on my routes."

"You could just run by the guy covering you?"

"Yeah, except those guys are almost as fast as I am now," Tristan said morosely. "It's going to be an adjustment."

"I know you've got this," Wade said, and believed it, because to do what Tristan had done from a young teenage age would've taken an incredible strength of purpose. And this? This was just football.

"We'd better get to the meeting," Tristan said, his gaze sliding away as he stood and picked up his tray. "Don't want to be late on our first day."

Tristan was not surprised when Wade took a seat in the front row of the auditorium. There were mostly only rookies here now—the veterans weren't required to be here for another few days—so there were about a hundred seats to pick from.

Of course Wade picked the front row.

He was that kind of upstanding, studying-hard, tell-it-like-it-is, my-handshake-is-law sort of guy.

He'd want to make a good first impression on Coach Dawson. After all, unlike every other player who'd given Beau Dawson a fairly wide berth, Wade had gotten to know him well enough at the optional workouts that they'd even developed a special hand-shake.

You are not jealous. Not even a little bit.

But watching Beau and Wade exchange waves as he and Coach walked into the room made it hard to dismiss that feeling entirely.

"Hey, y'all," Coach Dawson said in his trademark drawl.

Tristan, who'd been born in Washington, outside of Seattle, and had gone to school in Ohio, had spent a few somewhat embarrassing hours watching Coach give press conferences so he could decipher what the fuck he was saying. The last thing he'd wanted to do was get to camp and not be able to understand the head coach because of this thick Alabama accent.

That definitely wouldn't help him make the final roster.

Coach leaned a hip on the corner of a long table set up at the front of the auditorium. He was in his late forties, with the same dark hair as his son, except his was liberally streaked with silver. His skin was tanned leather hide, worn from so many years of sun exposure, and his eyes shone with a fierce intelligence that you couldn't miss, even though many thought he was an idiot because of the way he talked.

But Tristan knew it would be absolutely stupid to underestimate him.

"Welcome to Piranhas camp," Coach continued, "I'm real glad you're here, and I'm excited to get some work in. Be ready to work harder than you ever did in your whole life."

Beau nudged his dad. "You really tryin' to scare them off?"

But Coach just threw his head back and laughed. "They ain't scared," he said. "They're eager. But maybe they might be scared of your presentation. All those numbers, make their eyes cross."

Beau didn't look offended by this opinion, even as he rolled his eyes. "Sure, Coach."

"I wanna start this meetin' out by talking about expectations," Coach said, like his son hadn't said a word, "and what the expectations are for this upcoming season. I'm sure at thirty-one other camps out there, the coach is tellin' his rookies that they're gonna win the Super Bowl." Coach's eyes narrowed. "But I'm stupid. I'm not gonna tell you that. We're rebuilding a decimated team. You're the fresh blood we need. I want to stick around to do the work, to make the magic happen, to win that ring, but we gotta play our asses off this year to make that possible."

It was not what Tristan had expected Coach to say. It wasn't what *any* other coach in the NFL would've said. Coach Dawson was right, every other head coach would be standing up there, talking about the path to the Super Bowl.

"I wanna be good, but I know we aren't ready to be great yet," Coach continued. "But we're gonna get there. This is the first step to greatness." He glanced over at Beau. "You got the schedule, son?"

Beau leaned over and hit a few buttons on the laptop sitting on the table and the Piranhas logo appeared on the screen hanging in the back of the auditorium. He picked up a clicker from the table, and began to click through the slides.

The next one that appeared was a schedule.

There was a rumble that went through the group of rookies, even though there were only thirteen of them.

"Yep, it's a tough schedule," Coach drawled out. "Tough, maybe, but you're tough too, and I know you can handle it."

It *was* a tough schedule. Breakfast at six every day. Weights every other day. Followed by back-to-back-to-back meetings. Followed by lunch. Followed by two practices. Followed by dinner, and then a bunch more meetings.

There was a similarity to the schedule he'd had back in high school—that's when two-a-days had started, of course—and also to college—that's when the meetings had begun. But it was *way* more. All kinds of intensity wrapped up into a fourteen-hour day.

Tristan felt the back of his neck twitch and his palms go sweaty.

He wanted to believe he could do this, but facing it was an entirely different thing.

"We'll have you meet our coordinators and position coaches in a bit," Coach said. "But I wanted to take this time to really talk to you, man to man."

Tristan glanced over and Wade looked a little bit nervous but mostly enraptured.

Count him not only as the kind of guy whose handshake was ironclad, but who was probably masochistic enough to enjoy two-a-days.

"And," Beau added, "you've been working them to the bone back in Miami and you gave them the morning off."

Coach shot his son a half-hearted glare. "Don't be scared off, okay? Beau's just a teaser. I should mention, Beau here is my right-hand man. He's me, but younger and better lookin'. So if he asks you to do something . . ." Coach's eyes narrowed, and in the front row, Tristan found there was no way to miss their penetrating intensity. "It better get done. Beau's also a genius."

"Dad . . ." Beau interrupted, looking a little embarrassed.

"Don't Dad me," Coach retorted. "It's Coach to you, I'm your boss. And Beau might be a trifle modest, but he's still a genius. Anyone who wants to get ahead . . ." Tristan *swore* Coach looked right at him. Stupid Wade, wanting to sit in the front row. "Should really spend some time talkin' to him about football. He watches more film than well . . . anybody I know." Coach smiled. "Even me. So that's sayin' something. So, anybody have any questions for me? Or maybe for Beau?"

A guy a few rows back who Tristan vaguely recognized from the combine—maybe he was a defensive end or even a cornerback?—raised his hand. "Coach," he said, "is this schedule so intense because we're playing in the Hall of Fame game?"

"We do gotta be ready before anyone else," Coach Dawson said solemnly, "but the schedule is the way it is because we gotta be better than we're expected to be. Period. End of story."

Tristan didn't tend to listen to the sports media's constant revolving door of gossip and speculation, but even he had heard that nobody thought the Piranhas were going to be very good this year.

Obviously Coach had heard the same rumors and was determined to prove them wrong.

"You're all here because you've got the tool kit," Beau said, speaking up. "But it's got to be polished and refined. That's why this schedule is so tough. There's lots of work to be done."

"Speaking of work," Coach said, suddenly straightening. "I think it's time to put some in at the weight room. But, I mean it, my door's open. Beau's door is open. For anything," he added with a firm tone, "except complaints about how tough the work is. This is the NFL. You've got to be better—faster, stronger, more prepared—than the guy linin' up opposite you."

With that real gung ho pep talk, Beau turned off the laptop, and everyone began to file out to head to the weight room.

Tristan wanted to pretend the anxiety roiling in his gut was a figment of his imagination, but it was hard to, when he saw it in so many of the other guys' faces.

"Hey," he said under his breath as he and Wade headed towards the weight room, "did that surprise you any?"

"No," Wade said, and his eyes were already shining like a disciple. "Coach Dawson is a freaking genius."

"I thought that was supposed to be Beau," Tristan grumbled.

"Oh, him too," Wade said, looking no less starstruck as he thought about Beau. And that didn't disgruntle Tristan any. Nope, not a bit. "But Coach Dawson is a legend. I'm fortunate to play for him. You are too. He's gonna fix this team's problems. I hear he even brought in Randy Foreman, you know, the passing whisperer." Wade glanced down at Tristan. "You should be excited about this. There's always room for more people to catch the ball in Randy Foreman's systems."

But what if I can't?

That wasn't a voice Tristan had experienced much in his life.

He'd always shoved criticism and self-doubt aside. But having his play dissected and analyzed and found wanting in college had made that voice harder to ignore. All the times he'd been told that speed was all he brought to the table, those had sucked.

He wanted to do more. Be more.

But for the first time in a very long time, he wasn't sure he could.

"Don't worry," Wade said, dropping his voice further. "You've got this. And I've got you, okay?"

Tristan hoped he didn't look too surprised.

Sure, he and Wade were becoming friends. But they were still technically competing against each other. It would be easier for Wade if he just let Tristan flounder. It would mean there'd be one less person he'd have to compete against for a roster spot at the end of camp. But that clearly was not how Wade Lewis was made.

And Tristan, who already liked Wade a little too much, suddenly liked him even more.

It was a problem.

Wade was lifting on one of the stationary benches, curls and crunches with one of the bigger weights, his muscles bunching and releasing as he went through his reps, the strength and conditioning coach talking him through it.

That wasn't the problem so much as he was doing it shirtless and it was doing things to Tristan's insides.

Things that were so distracting he was finding it tough to focus on his quad reps.

"Nicholson," Niko, the assistant strength and conditioning coach, barked at him. "Heads up. Get those reps done. You're dawdling."

He totally was dawdling, and he flushed bright red, hating that he'd just been called out on it.

Eight years playing football and he'd never let the obvious physical attributes of another player distract him like this.

But then, he'd never seen a player quite like Wade before.

He was so big and wide and so fucking strong. The way the muscles rippled under his skin, the gleam of the sweat, the way he gritted his teeth and worked for that next rep . . . *God*, it made Tristan weak in the knees. Which, when he was trying to work on his leg strength, was a real fucking problem.

"On it," Tristan muttered under his breath, pulling his eyes away from Wade and focusing instead on the South Orange poster on the wall. Reminding himself that this was where he'd started—playing Division III ball—and he was trying to make it in the NFL, something that very few players had ever done before.

If he wanted to make it happen, if he wanted to reach the peak of his possibilities, then he needed to fucking focus.

He made it through the rest of his reps, and Niko gave him a begrudging nod. "Good job," he said, tossing Tristan a towel. "You're coming along."

Tristan didn't feel like he was coming along. He thought he'd come into camp in great shape, but after an hour in the weight room, he definitely had gotten the impression that he wasn't quite as far along as anyone would've wanted.

Chalk that up to his ankle injury and missing those critical few weeks.

"Let's work on your core," Niko said, gesturing to the mat. He pulled out a medicine ball, demonstrated the first exercise that he wanted Tristan to do.

Just think, he thought as he got through the first set of reps, *of the great fucking six-pack you'll have when this is over. You'll get any guy you want, just by taking your shirt off.*

The rest of the sets were even worse than the first, and by the end he was sweating, fingers slipping on the ball, grinding his teeth against the pain. But he did it, he made it through, and there was undeniably respect on Niko's face.

Then Tristan leveraged himself up, abs aching, and came face-to-face with a shirtless, sweaty Wade.

A *smiling* Wade.

Yeah, he was definitely that masochistic sort that actually *enjoyed* the torture.

Tristan didn't get it, and he wasn't sure he ever would.

"Hey," Tristan said.

He grabbed a towel and wiped down his face. Because as attractive as a sweaty Wade was, Tristan was pretty sure it wasn't that good of a look on him. He could only imagine how red and flushed he was.

"Feels good, doesn't it?" Wade asked as they walked over to the water station.

"No, it feels like hell," Tristan grumbled. "You're one of those annoying exercise endorphin people, aren't you?"

"Yep," Wade proclaimed happily.

Tristan was marginally less annoyed because a Wade flooded with endorphins was undeniably adorable.

"And hey, Niko wouldn't be bothering to work you that hard if he thought you couldn't make the team," Wade said, leaning in closer—and not only was he that annoying type that enjoyed exercise, he was the even more annoying type that never seemed to smell bad after it, just more like himself, a scent that Tristan was becoming familiar with because every time he walked into the room they shared, he was wrapped in it.

Something woodsy and elemental, like the forest after a rainstorm, ozone crackling and the moss damp with moisture.

"True," Tristan said. He hadn't thought about that. Hadn't been able to think of much else except the work and the pain.

"Just saying," Wade teased, his damp hair pushed back from his forehead, his light gray eyes twinkling irrepressibly, his face suddenly very near to Tristan's own.

And Tristan, who considered himself a fairly intelligent person, felt himself rocked by the very strong, nearly irresistible desire to reach up on his tiptoes and press his mouth against Wade's.

He wanted to know, nearly as much as he wanted his next breath, if Wade tasted just as good as he smelled.

Wade's lips curled further upwards, and his eyes impossibly growing warmer, as they inched closer together.

Like he wanted it just as much as Tristan did, which was impossible, because Tristan wanted it a whole hell of a lot.

The only thing that stopped him was how incredibly stupid it would be. He'd torpedo his chances to make the Piranhas almost definitely. Kissing Wade was probably a mistake no matter what, but kissing Wade in the weight room, with all these guys around?

Stupid, certainly, and also the kind of careless that Tristan had never been. Wade had trusted him with his secret. He hadn't trusted any of these other guys, and what kind of LGBTQ advocate would he be if he outed Wade like that?

Not a very good one.

Certainly not a very respectful one.

It was just enough reality to toss a bucketful of cold water in Tristan's face. He turned and gulped down half a cupful of Gatorade.

Hoped that it not only restored his energy but his sanity, too.

Wade didn't say anything, but Tristan could still feel his eyes on him.

If he looked over now, would Wade be confused? Questioning? Upset? Maybe he would look just the same as before, like he hadn't realized what was happening.

That, Tristan decided, was the best course of action.

To pretend it hadn't happened at all.

"Come on," Tristan said, forcing his voice to sound casual and light, like they hadn't almost just kissed in the Piranhas weight room, "let's grab some lunch and get ready for practice."

"Yeah, I'll meet you there." Wade, clearly, had not spent as much time as Tristan perfecting that tone, and he sounded slightly perturbed still.

Like he wasn't sure what had just happened.

Well, that, Tristan thought, as he headed towards the cafeteria, makes two of us.

Tristan wouldn't say he avoided Wade for the rest of the day—after all, they ate lunch together, and walked to practice together, and hung out and watched TV in the common room together between practices, and then walked to a *second* practice together—but he also made sure they weren't alone.

He didn't want Wade to ask him what was going on, because he didn't know how to answer that question.

He was so tempted to tell Wade the truth: *we're attracted to each other, and I want to kiss you, and I think you may want to kiss me, and that's a disaster in the making, you know that as well as I do.*

But admitting they might be attracted to each other, it was practically tantamount to allowing it to happen—and then allowing it to continue.

Tristan already knew, had spent every spare moment when he wasn't occupied with football, telling himself that it couldn't continue.

He'd nearly found Beau and asked if he could switch rooms, but the problem with that was that he *liked* sharing a room with Wade. He was a good roommate, conscientious and kind, and apart from this inconvenient attraction stuff, he was becoming a good friend.

And he'd already been around the NFL long enough to know that friends didn't exactly grow on trees.

It shouldn't have come as a surprise, then, that as soon as the light went out, after this long-ass day, when both of them should have been exhausted and immediately falling asleep, Tristan couldn't help himself and instead of being safe and smart and careful, like he had been all day, like he'd used all that safety up, he asked the question himself.

"You ever kiss a guy before, Wade?"

Wade was quiet for such a long time that Tristan wondered if maybe he *had* actually fallen asleep.

He found himself holding his breath, barely able to breathe, his lungs clogging, as he waited for Wade to answer. Listening, way too intently, for even the minutest change in Wade's own breathing.

Why did he even need to know?

Why did it matter so much that the answer be no?

Finally, Wade let out a deep exhale, like he'd been holding his own breath too. Like he'd made a decision.

"No," he said. "No, I haven't."

Tristan dug his fingertips into his bedding. It was no less dangerous to kiss Wade in this dark, private room than to do it in the middle of the day, in the middle of the Piranhas weight room, but it was easier to justify because if they did it here and now, nobody would ever know.

But you'd know, Tristan reminded himself. *And Wade will know.*

It was those two things that kept Tristan in his own bed, instead of joining Wade in his—and showing him just how great kissing a guy could be.

"Is . . . is that what that was earlier? You were . . ." Wade hesitated for so long that Tristan, hanging on every single word, every single syllable echoing through the darkness, nearly got up and went to his side and demanded to know what it was he was supposedly doing. Finally, though, Wade finished his sentence. "Testing me?"

It made no sense. Why would Tristan be testing him? He already knew Wade was bisexual. Wade had told him himself. Tristan might have tested Wade if he hadn't been sure. If he hadn't been entirely sure how his flirtation would be received.

But he definitely hadn't been testing Wade earlier.

He'd been irresistibly drawn to the man.

It felt unfair to pay Wade's honesty back with a lie, no matter how dangerous the truth was.

So Tristan told him the truth.

"I wasn't testing you. I was . . . if you have to know, I was . . . I find you attractive, Wade, and I wanted to kiss you. As stupid as that was. I shouldn't have been thinking about it. You're not out, and there were other guys around, and on top of that . . . it's a huge, massive distraction that could get us both released. You know, teams don't really like their players hooking up."

Don't really was an understatement.

It was technically allowed because it couldn't be *not* allowed but it certainly wasn't encouraged. All the Piranhas needed was a really good reason to cut Tristan, and this would be it.

"You wanted to kiss me?" Wade's voice was full of wonder.

"I guess you missed the rest of that," Tristan teased. "You know, the part where it was—it *is*—a bad idea."

"Sorry." Wade actually sounded apologetic. "I got stuck on that one bit. I just never thought . . . you and me. You're so . . ."

It was playing with fire to ask.

Tristan knew it.

He asked anyway.

"I'm so what, Wade?"

"You're so hot and confident and sure of yourself. You're a beacon of hope to so many closeted guys, guys who think that you can't be gay and play football. And then there's me . . . not really ashamed but not open either, and not experienced . . ."

"None of that matters," Tristan interrupted him, because he couldn't listen to another moment of Wade putting himself down. "I can't tell you how much none of that matters."

"It doesn't?"

"Wade, you're fucking gorgeous and you're sweet, and you've got this smile that lights up . . . well, it lights up everything around you. Including me, okay?"

Wade was silent for a long time again, like he was digesting what Tristan had just admitted to.

Like he was weighing the danger of it, the inherent risk of it, with the reward.

But how could he, Tristan thought, dying over in his own bed, when he didn't know what he was really missing? He'd never kissed a guy before. He didn't *know*.

"Why," Wade said, his voice rough, "are you still over there, then?"

Tristan laughed, a little hysterically. Why was he over there?

"I don't know," he said. "Self-preservation? The persistent idea that this might be a mistake that neither of us can take back?"

"Anyone ever tell you that you think way too much?" Wade's tone was amused, and it was suddenly a lot closer, like he was moving across the room, and yeah, those were definitely his foot-steps on the floor.

Tristan's breath seized in his lungs.

Trust Wade, once he knew what he wanted was mutual, to go right after it.

He'd been squeezing his eyes shut, probably against the inherent temptation, but when he opened them, there Wade was, right next to his bed. Tristan could see the outline of him, clad in a t-shirt and a pair of boxer briefs, and could see him shift his weight from one foot to another. Like he was nervous.

Tristan was nervous too, his breath coming in short choppy pants, his pulse accelerating, but the nerves were quickly being overtaken by anticipation.

He was going to get to kiss Wade Lewis.

He was going to be Wade Lewis' first kiss with a guy.

Pushing himself up, ignoring the soreness in his body, he put a hand on Wade's shoulder, and squeezed the solid muscle there. "We don't have to do anything you don't want to," Tristan said.

Figured that since he had the most experience here, he should also be the voice of reason.

But Wade didn't respond.

At least not with words.

He leaned down, and carefully, gently, like Tristan would spook—and *Wade* was the one with the lack of experience here!—pressed his lips against Tristan's.

It was sweeter and so much softer than Tristan had expected it would be.

Then he twisted himself, raising himself higher, closer to Wade, and slid his fingers around his shoulder, to his neck and gripped, and the change of angle changed everything.

Tristan fell headfirst into Wade and everything he was.

The way he smelled, the way his mouth moved, the settled confidence in the way he cupped Tristan's head with his palms and kissed him just the way he wanted to.

Heat raced through Tristan's veins as Wade took little sips of him, deeper and deeper each time, until suddenly they were gulping each other, Wade's tongue delving into his mouth.

It was the wildest kiss Tristan had ever had, enough to bring him right to the edge, his cock throbbing in his briefs, underneath his pajama pants, and it was Wade's first goddamn kiss with a guy.

But the inexperience didn't matter, because either Wade *knew* how to kiss, or else it was the two of them together, the chemistry he'd felt from the first moment he'd turned around and seen the man with his own two eyes, catching fire and burning them both.

Wade pulled away, right before Tristan lost his mind and went for his cock.

It would be too much. All Tristan had asked for was a kiss, even though he'd never technically *asked*.

The question had been there, in the air between them, since this morning. But the last thing Tristan wanted was to scare him away.

It had been too good.

He could hear Wade's sharp intake of breath. How he couldn't quite catch it.

Could still taste Wade on his bottom lip.

Wanted to taste it some more.

"So," Tristan said, because Wade was *right*, he did think—and talk—too much, "how was that?"

Wade gave a short disbelieving laugh. "You really don't have to ask, do you?"

"No, but my ego always likes an extra boost," Tristan said.

"I just bet it does." Wade sounded deeply, darkly amused.

"Do you want to know what else it likes?"

They were definitely playing with fire now.

Tristan knew it, but he couldn't tear his hands away.

He wanted them all over the man in front of him.

"What?" Wade asked.

"You," Tristan said. And then it was him reaching up, tangling his fingers in Wade's short hair, and pulling him down, their mouths mashing together in another incendiary kiss.

Chapter Three

Wade was tired.

Every other guy here was no doubt feeling the same bone-deep exhaustion he was. Yesterday had been really, really long, no question about it.

But then, Wade thought holding back another yawn, they hadn't spent another extra hour after they were supposed to be asleep, making out with the hottest guy in the universe.

Tristan's eyes were droopy, clearly just as tired as Wade was, but he looked so pleased with himself, it obviously wasn't bothering him much.

"It's six in the morning," Tristan said, "what can you possibly be grinning about?"

Wade's cheeks were aching from how much he was smiling.

It wasn't like Tristan's smile wasn't just as bright. Because it was. Like he couldn't stop either.

"Uh, well . . . there's this guy. A super cute guy. We kissed last night." Wade dropped his voice down to barely above a whisper. It wasn't like he didn't agree with Tristan; this *was* a distraction and he wasn't stupid enough to believe that the coaches wouldn't use it as an excuse if either of them didn't play quite well enough. But he also had every intention of playing his ass off, no matter how much he enjoyed kissing Tristan—and he knew Tristan could be just as good as he was, if not better.

There was no reason for them to be sent home early.

Whether they spent the evenings kissing or not.

"Did you really?" Tristan's mouth twisted into an adorable smirk. It made Wade want to lean forward and kiss it right off him.

He didn't. He might be crushing hard, but he wasn't stupid.

Kissing Tristan hadn't been like kissing anyone else. Not just because he was a guy, though that did make it different. No, kissing Tristan was unique and amazing and incredible because it was *Tristan*. He had so much life and light and fire inside him, and it all poured out of him whenever their mouths touched.

Wade nodded. "Yep, it was totally unlike me, but that wasn't even the best part about it."

He didn't know what the best part had been: was it how eagerly Tristan had melted into him when he'd touched him for the first time, or how respectful he'd been? He'd clearly felt Wade's own erection, and he'd felt Tristan's in return, but there had been zero pressure to do anything about it. It was the first time in years that Wade had kissed only to kiss, and it had been fucking amazing.

Tristan's eyes gleamed. "What was the best part?"

"That we can do it again, tonight."

Tristan laughed. "Maybe if we take a nap during afternoon break."

"I won't be able to stay awake, even if I wanted to," Wade confessed.

He was tired.

But it was the best kind of tired.

"Come on," Tristan said, picking up his coffee. "Let's get to our first meeting."

It was one thing to stay awake at practice, it was entirely another to do it during meetings—which they had a full morning of.

After the morning meeting, during which Beau had presented a mind-numbing number of statistical slides, they'd broken out to offensive and defensive meetings.

Randy Foreman was the offensive pass coordinator, who would be coordinating between Davis Abernathy, the quarterbacks coach, and the wide receivers and the tight ends, in an attempt to make the Piranhas' passing game the most dynamic and successful it could be.

Wade had never had a pass coordinator before, but he already liked Randy, who had both a laid-back attitude and a detailed work ethic.

He sat on the corner of the table in front of the smaller conference room, and instead of a lengthy and confusing PowerPoint presentation, he just *talked* to the players.

"I want this to be a collaborative effort," Coach Randy said. "If something isn't working for you guys, I wanna know about it, right away. My door's open. And I don't just say that as fucking PR bullshit, okay? I mean it. We've got talent up the ass here. Pax Norwood is a dynamite QB, a once-in-a-lifetime talent, who despite this team tanking last year, played his fucking ass off."

Coach Randy's eyes narrowed as Tristan yawned—for the third time, Wade totally wasn't keeping track except he couldn't help it, he was *so* painfully aware of every single time Tristan shifted in the chair next to him.

"Am I boring you, Nicholson?"

Tristan jerked up straight. "No, no, of course not. Definitely not. Paxton is great. I can't wait to catch some of his balls."

Coach Randy's mouth quirked up. "He's a fucking artist, that's for sure. And he's got the arm strength if you let him air it out. You're fast enough, Nicholson. Might even be able to keep up with you."

"I plan on making him work for it, Coach," Tristan said earnestly.

"Good." Coach Randy nodded. He stood and went back to the whiteboard that was on the back wall. "Let's talk about the game plan for this year. Like the overall shit, the shit that's going to win us some games."

When his back turned and he began to outline a general game plan with a black and a red marker, Tristan muffled another yawn behind his hand, and when he looked over, his eyes were tired but twinkling.

Wade forced his attention back to the play that Coach Randy was drawing up because this wasn't like the classes he hadn't liked in college; this was serious, this was the rest of his life. He couldn't let Tristan distract him from this.

Besides, the more Coach Randy drew, the more Wade liked it. It was an ambitious game plan, with lots of complex crossing routes, and if he wasn't mistaken, even some with tight ends running wide receiver routes, which he'd never gotten to do, even at Michigan.

It helped him push some of his tiredness aside, and when they broke to make their way to the locker room for the first practice of the day, he found he couldn't get dressed fast enough.

"Did you see that route that Coach mapped out last?" Tristan was clearly excited too, his voice high and his words tumbling out fast. "I think if I can run the route the way he said, seamless the way he talked about, we're talking *deep* passes, and I know Pax can throw them."

"Pax?" Wade teased as he pulled his gloves on. "You and QB1 on a first-name basis now?"

First practice of the day was always a walk-through—focused more on execution, which meant that they got to forgo pads—and the defensive hits that added to the wear and tear on their bodies.

Last season had been Paxton Kelly's rookie year, and he'd come out of USC as one of the best college quarterbacks in recent years. Of course, he'd been drafted to the Miami Piranhas as a replacement for the legendary Colin O'Connor, who'd just retired after winning the Super Bowl. Unfortunately for Pax, much of that team had left or retired, and last year had been a disaster.

He'd been one of the sole positives in a year full of failures. But even that hadn't been enough to bolster Paxton Kelly's confidence. It had waned, towards the end of the year, and he'd ended up throwing almost as many interceptions as he had touchdowns.

It was part of why the Piranhas had brought in Asa Dawson—he was supposed to be a defensive genius, and also the best at getting the most out of his players—but also why the expectations for this upcoming season were low.

Nobody thought with a bunch of rookies and has-beens that they could do much better than the year before.

"I met him while I was out in LA, working out with Alec's guys," Tristan said. "He's working with Heath, on the offseason, you know, on a strictly off-the-books way. Probably because Sam asked him. You know, Sam went to USC." It was a perfectly reasonable explanation, and yet, Wade was fairly certain that was a blush on Tristan's face.

Wade told himself not to be jealous, because the guy who'd be kissing Tristan tonight was going to be him, not Paxton Kelly, but it was tougher than he'd imagined to dismiss.

Probably why teams highly discouraged players hooking up; locker rooms were volatile enough without adding sexual tension and personal jealousy to the mix.

"He's a cool guy, then?"

"Oh yeah, totally. Really fucking good quarterback. He threw me a few balls, you know, just to air it out, and wow, he's got an arm."

"So you *do* know the answer to Coach Randy's question. You can totally match your speed to his arm strength."

Tristan blushed again, and then looked away as they walked through the tunnel out onto the field. It was weird, and Wade told himself he was being stupid, but he resisted the urge to ask what was bothering him.

But because Tristan was Tristan, he told Wade anyway. "He told me I needed to run a better route," he said, and there were shades of embarrassment in his voice. "Said I'd been doing fine in Division III, but I'd need to be a lot better to make it in the NFL."

"You're gonna get there," Wade said.

Maybe Tristan had said that Pax was a good guy, but Wade was beginning to think he was kind of an asshole.

Tristan wasn't going to get there overnight, and by discouraging him before he already began? He wasn't ever going to make it there.

"I guess we'll see," Tristan said lightly, clearly wanting to dismiss his own worries, but Wade stopped and tugged on Tristan's shoulder, right when the sideline met the field, and pulled him around to face him.

"No," Wade said. "You are what you believe. You want to believe the bullshit that Paxton's spouting? Well, then it'll happen.

You won't be good enough. You want to make the team? Believe that you will, and you'll figure out a way to make it reality."

Tristan's smile was small, but genuine. "I . . . I guess you're right. I need to do more visualizations, I know that."

"You do and you *will*. We'll do them together," Wade promised.

And then Coach Randy was beckoning them over.

"Let's get stretched and warmed up," Coach said, shoving his hands in his pockets. "Pax won't be here for a few days, but Abernathy's here, and he can toss you guys some balls."

Wade was not proud of how he gawked. "Davis Abernathy?"

"He *is* the quarterbacks coach, and back in the day, he was a damn good quarterback himself."

"Only the best quarterback since Dan Marino never to win the Super Bowl," Wade said.

Coach laughed, and patted Wade on the shoulder. "Just don't tell him that, okay? He's . . . well, he's a mite sensitive about that subject."

"Understandable," Tristan said, nodding enthusiastically. "Well, I'm plenty happy to catch some passes from him. He's a legend."

"Well, get warmed up and we'll see what you can do," Coach Randy said.

Wade and Tristan went over to where the rest of the offensive rookies were stretching. Niko was there, leading them in a series of warmup exercises.

Wade picked a nice patch of grass and followed along, feeling his sore muscles begin to unwind and stretch out.

He'd been working out before and after the combine, sometimes it felt like nonstop but it was going to feel so good to get back on the field with his team and actually run some plays.

Plays that they'd run in actual games.

Plays that could result in first downs and touchdowns.

Wade looked up and Tristan was smiling too, quietly, to himself, like he'd felt the same thing, and Wade was suddenly really glad that he'd met him.

Not just because of the kissing, but because they got each other.

They weren't really anything alike, but they weren't all that different either.

"I can't fucking believe that my first practice out, I totally fuck it up."

Tristan wanted to tell Wade that he hadn't, not really, but it was impossible to ignore that he hadn't run the first route particularly well—or any of the subsequent routes, either.

And then there were the dropped passes.

It was not surprising for wide receivers and tight ends, and sometimes even running backs, to drop one pass and then keep on dropping them.

You started overthinking and overanalyzing and trying so hard to make sure it didn't happen again that it *kept* happening again.

Without much of a break in between the plays in question, Tristan knew there hadn't been time for Wade to regroup. The coaches, probably wanting to see what kind of stuff he was really made of, when the going got tough, pushed him hard.

"Again," Coach Randy had called out over and over, his laid-back voice suddenly hard around the edges.

Wade had dropped probably ninety percent of the passes and the routes he'd run had been bad.

Tristan, who'd secretly worried that he would end up in that position, exposed and at the mercy of the coaches, had only been able to watch in disbelief as Wade had been the one who'd struggled.

Tristan himself had had a really nice fifty-yard pass, catching the ball from Davis Abernathy, who'd given the ball the right kind of light touch he was always known for in his passing game.

Coach Randy had given him an approving nod, and while Tristan had been pleased, relieved almost, he hadn't missed Wade's scowl.

Tristan wasn't stupid enough to think Wade was mad at him.

No, Wade was mad at himself.

The coaches weren't very happy with him either.

For a moment, Tristan considered telling him that he didn't completely fuck it up, but it wouldn't be the truth.

He could fix it, but it was undeniably completely fucked up right now.

"You can come out in the next practice this afternoon, and you can show them that you can conquer this," Tristan said, leaning forward over the table. They were in the cafeteria, supposedly to eat and chill before the afternoon's next practice, but Wade wasn't eating.

In fact, all Wade seemed capable of doing was staring, grim-faced, at the full plate in front of him.

"I'm not sure I can get out of my own fucking way," Wade grumbled.

Tristan leaned back in his chair. "Listen, and I say this with all the love in the world, but eat your fucking sandwich, and relax, or you're going to be right, there's no way you'll be able to get out of your own way."

Wade shot him a half-hearted glare.

"Yes," Tristan said, "you hate that I'm right. I know. But seriously. Eat your goddamned sandwich, okay? It's gonna be fine."

"You don't have to do this, you know," Wade grumbled. But he picked up the sandwich.

"Do what?" Tristan played with the cap of his Gatorade. He wasn't trying to play coy. He usually wasn't very good at it. But he knew he needed to do something to jerk Wade out of this bad mood.

"Help me," Wade said baldly. Like he hadn't been encouraging and helping Tristan since the first day.

"Why wouldn't I?"

"We're technically competing for a spot, as you like to remind me," Wade said.

"Yeah, but here's the thing. We're not here as roster fodder. You especially. There's what . . . room for ten players per position on the initial ninety-two-man roster, right? Or that's what my agent is always telling me. So there's ten spots, there's room for four or five on the actual, fifty-three-man roster. One or two in the middle, right on the bubble, and then there's another handful on the back end, who are just here as roster fodder. You're not here for that. You were the Piranhas' second-round draft pick. You're here to make the team, Wade."

Wade didn't say anything for a long moment. Instead, he took several bites of his sandwich, chewed and then swallowed them.

Then he set it down.

"You," he drawled, "are not just a pretty face."

"Aw, you think I'm pretty?" Tristan teased.

Wade had the nerve to flush, which made him somehow even cuter than he had been before. Tristan had been worried before now that he was going to slide in deep. But now, he knew it was going to happen, and he couldn't find it in himself to give a shit anymore.

"You know you're pretty," Wade said.

"Yeah, but now I know that *you* know I'm pretty."

Wade laughed then, and that was all Tristan had wanted to accomplish. To relax him. To get him out of his own head. To make him realize that he could do this, if he stopped overanalyzing every single move he'd made.

"I don't know how you did that," Wade admitted sheepishly. "How *did* you do that?"

Tristan shrugged. "It's a gift, but you were an easy nut to crack."

"An easy nut to crack?" Wade raised an eyebrow as he lifted his sandwich again.

Tristan had hooked up with enough hot guys in his high school and then college life that he shouldn't be blushing.

Except he was, because there was a knowing glint in Wade's eyes, and Tristan had a feeling that no matter how frustrated and angry he was, the moment they were in their room, and the lights were off, Wade was going to be all over him.

Tristan had been trying to give him space. Trying to be patient.

After all, last night was the first night he'd ever kissed a guy.

But he felt itchy and distracted, the arousal humming just under his skin whenever he and Wade even looked at each other. And when they touched . . . well, he couldn't even think about that. Not right now.

If he needed to go without an orgasm for another night, he could do it—but only if he excused himself to the bathroom after their make-out session.

"It's just . . . it's just an expression," Tristan stuttered.

When he was usually so confident and charming and got what he wanted just by turning a bright smile onto an unsuspecting guy.

But Wade fucked him up.

Wade had fucked him up from the first moment they'd met.

Wade leaned in, sandwich forgotten again on his plate. "Does it *have* to be just an expression?"

"No, it doesn't, but—"

Tristan didn't get the rest of his sentence out before Wade interrupted him. "I don't want it to be just an expression," he said bluntly. "I liked it. I want more. If you're okay with that."

Tristan couldn't hold back his nervous chuckle.

Tried to remember when he used to wrap hot guys around his little finger, effortlessly.

This hot guy had wrapped *him* around his finger, pretty damn effortlessly from where Tristan was standing.

"I'm definitely okay with that."

"Alright." Wade hesitated, picking up his sandwich again. "I didn't know if you wanted . . ."

"I wanted." Tristan said it with all the confidence that he could muster. "I definitely wanted."

Wade's smile was slow and sweet and seared Tristan. "I thought so, but I thought it'd be good to check," he drawled.

Tristan leaned back in his chair. "Finish your sandwich and stop trying to get me to run to the bathroom before our next practice starts, okay?"

"Am I doing that?" Wade's gray eyes were guileless, but Tristan couldn't miss the heat in them.

He knew exactly what the fuck he was doing.

"You're doing that." Tristan squirmed in his chair. "And it's hot and it's annoying, okay?"

"Well, just so we're on the same page, then, because you just charmed the fuck out of me."

"I got you out of your own head," Tristan corrected gently. But he *had*, all in an attempt to do that. To distract Wade from what had happened at the earlier practice. To try to get him to forget it had happened, and to focus on building his confidence so that the mistakes wouldn't repeat themselves at the next.

"Either way, I appreciate it," Wade said, his voice deep and rumbly.

Reminding Tristan of just how it had felt to swallow Wade's groans last night.

Frankly, both of them needed to think way less about last night—and about the upcoming night—and way more about the upcoming practice that could potentially make or break their careers.

"I'm gonna go splash some cold water on my face," Tristan said, standing up. "Finish your sandwich, and I'll meet you in one of the small rooms, to study those plays before practice starts, okay?"

Wade glanced up, those light, clear eyes narrowing. "Just your face?" he asked, his voice surprisingly sharp.

For a second, Tristan didn't realize what he was asking and then, *oh*, he remembered what he'd said just five minutes before, about needing to go to the bathroom to relieve a certain kind of pressure.

. .

"Just my face," Tristan said firmly, resting a hand on Wade's shoulder as he passed by him on the way to the bathroom. "I promise."

Wade breathed in and then breathed out, centering himself, and then the whistle blew, and he pushed off, churning his legs as fast as they would go. He pushed off the defensive end, blocking squarely in the center of his pads. The guy had at least fifty pounds on Wade, and it was all muscle, but Wade was quicker on his feet, and lighter too, and he had the jump on him, which always made blocking so much easier.

The internal play clock in his head counted down, *one Mississippi, two Mississippi, three Mississippi*, and Davis popped back, ball in his hand, still solidly in the pocket.

Out of the corner of his eye, Wade saw Tristan streak past him, past the defense, a poor, beleaguered cornerback trying to keep up with him, and Wade counted out a *four Mississippi* and Davis let the ball fly, hitting Tristan's hands for a solid twenty-five-yard gain.

It was a good play. Made even better, Wade could admit, without feeling even the tiniest bit bitter, with him blocking on it.

But he wanted to do more than just blocking.

He was capable of more than just blocking.

Coach Randy knew it, but he was holding him back, pushing him off, not letting him do anything else other than block in this afternoon's practice with the helmets and pads on.

Clearly, the morning was weighing not just on Wade's mind, but Coach's too.

Wade got it.

Coach didn't want to create a pattern for him. Make him underestimate himself.

But he had this.

Tristan had distracted him just enough, and he was ready to try again. Could feel that same pass, hitting *him* square in the hands.

The cornerback had caught up to Tristan right after he'd caught it—he'd been forced to slow just enough because even though Wade would rather have died than admit it out loud, but Davis hadn't let the ball fly quite soon enough—and tackled him to the ground.

But Wade already knew he could've powered through that tackle.

He was stronger and bigger than Tristan.

He'd have turned that twenty-five-yard catch into a sixty-yard catch and run. Maybe even a touchdown. It would've erased the bad feeling in his mouth from this morning. Definitely would've erased Coach Randy's.

Coach blew the whistle, and Wade watched as the cornerback offered Tristan a hand up.

They both jogged back to the huddle, and Coach Randy was there again, getting ready to give them the next play.

In a real game or in a normal practice it might be a run play, especially since they'd just had a decent pass play, but because Coach Randy was the pass coordinator, Wade knew it wasn't going to be.

They'd be passing all afternoon.

And damn it all to hell if he was going to spend it blocking when he could be doing so much more.

"Coach," Wade said as he approached the huddle, "I've got this."

"Course you do, Lewis, you picked up that block, smooth as butter. I'm impressed."

"I can do more," Wade argued more.

It was not usually wise to argue with coaches. Especially coaches you were trying to make a good impression on. Coaches you were trying to convince to select you for their final roster.

But Coach couldn't do that if he didn't know what Wade was capable of.

Sure, he'd seen loads of film, and Wade's performance at the combine, but there was nothing like watching it unfold in front of you.

So he pushed. Hoping that he wasn't making a mistake.

"I can catch too. I know I didn't earlier, but I'm solid now."

Coach Randy glanced over at him. Kept looking, like he was searching for something in Wade's face. "You sure about that, Lewis?"

"I'm sure." Knew it was true, because if he doubted for even a second, he'd lose it all over again.

"Good." Coach gave him a nod, and then called out the play. Same play as before. Which meant that it would be twice as tough to repeat even the same success, because the defense would know exactly what it looked like, and what was coming.

Coach was testing him.

And Wade didn't intend to let him down.

"Nicholson, let's see if you can block as well as Wade here can," Coach said, "and, Wade, let's see if you can lose the protection."

"I can do it," Wade said.

The play unfolded exactly like it had before, except this time, Wade didn't stay near the pocket to block, he left that job to Tristan, and instead he took off, running at full speed past the first line of the defense, the corner trailing him the whole way, shadowing his movements.

Wade knew the general route, but he made a slight adjustment, a cut to the left, and then he saw the ball leave Davis' arm, a fucking beautiful spiral, and he adjusted again, just enough that the ball should just fall into his outstretched hands.

For a split second—it took longer to have the thought than to dismiss it—he overthought the play. What if he'd made the wrong adjustment? What if Davis threw the ball perfectly and he still missed it?

But those questions were already gone, and a second later, the ball fell into his waiting hands.

This time, he'd ditched the corner with his route, not his speed, and he wasn't around to tackle him.

So instead Wade plowed forward, sidestepping around the safety with a quick stiff arm—guys always underestimated how strong Wade was even though they'd been *warned*, and he could always overwhelm them with it, at least at first, and this one went right down, just like Wade had hoped he would.

It was easy enough to jog the rest of the fifteen yards to the end zone.

He spiked the ball, feeling the rush of success sweep through him.

Tristan was the first to get to the end zone with him, unsurprisingly, and he jumped into his arms.

It was a normal reaction to a touchdown.

Wade had participated in a hundred touchdown celebrations.

But he'd never had one before with a guy that he'd kissed before.

With a guy that he intended to kiss again.

For a split second, he hesitated, fingertips digging into Tristan's sides, and then he was down and Davis was jogging up, shaking his head. "That was some sweet running," he said. "And that stiff-arm? Brutal."

"Just the way I like it," Wade said.

And Tristan laughed.

Chapter Four

Wade knew he could front, and pretend that he wasn't eager as hell to get back to the room he shared with Tristan tonight—but he wasn't all that good at pretending. Especially when Tristan seemed to be just as eager as he was, deflecting several requests to hang out and play cards with some of the other guys, or watch a movie.

Or God forbid, watch more film with Coach Randy and Davis.

"Pax is getting in tonight, he said to keep it hot for him," Davis said, chuckling.

"Sounds like Pax, but neither of us are that crazy," Tristan had said with a reluctant laugh. "We'll leave you to it."

Triumph over such a fucking great practice was surging through his veins, with all its accompanying adrenaline, and the second Tristan closed their door, Wade pushed him up against it.

Laughter bubbled up out of Tristan's throat and Wade wanted to kiss it off his lips.

"Eager, are we?" Tristan teased, stroking a hand down Wade's scruffy cheek. "I like it."

He was. He was also a little nervous. He'd never done anything like this before, and Tristan clearly had. The last thing he wanted was to screw it up, before anything could even happen.

"I . . ." Wade flushed at how he stuttered. All it took was Tristan touching him—not just on the cheek but in the half a dozen places their bodies were pressed together.

"It's alright," Tristan said, his eyes glowing bright blue.

"Is it?" Wade didn't know. He pressed his fingertips into Tristan's hips. Pleading him without words to make it alright.

His blood was still hot, he was still fucking burning for him. But the fear was there too, and he couldn't dismiss it.

Tristan stared at him for a long second, but instead of answering, he reached up and pressed his mouth against Wade's.

They kissed for a long second, and the heat between them was almost enough to push the fear away.

But then, right as Wade began to lose himself in it, tilting his head so he could go deeper, fall further, Tristan pulled away.

"That," he said, hand reaching around Wade's neck, the heat of him searing, "is all we have to do."

"Kissing? But . . ."

"I know, but don't worry about it." Tristan paused, smiling. "Yes, I can see your worry. It's right here, in the crease between your eyebrows." He tapped the spot with his fingers. "And I don't want you to be worrying."

"I was, a little," Wade confessed.

Tristan pressed a single kiss against his mouth, then broke away again, surprising Wade by evading his grasp and heading over to his bed. "But you weren't last night, right?"

Wade followed—because he couldn't help himself. "No."

"Well, then, come sit down and we won't think—or worry—for awhile."

It was so easy to do as Tristan said, and the moment he did, he had his arms full, Tristan shedding his shoes, climbing into his arms.

It was also just as easy as it had been last night, once he'd taken the leap and kissed Tristan for the first time. As their mouths moved together, easy and slow at first, growing hotter and more intense in such tiny increments that he didn't even realize what was happening.

It took Tristan moaning, right into Wade's mouth, to realize what he was doing.

Yep, that was definitely his cock, and it was hard and aching, pressing against Tristan's hip, and yep, he'd definitely been thrusting.

Tristan's mouth was red and wet, his eyes dazed and unfocused, but he was smiling. He looked delighted, in fact.

"It's okay," Tristan said reassuringly. He adjusted himself in his own shorts, and yeah, okay, Wade wasn't the only one really fucking turned on, if the outline of Tristan's cock was any indication.

And *oh God*, that was Tristan's cock.

And it was hard.

For him.

"See, that wrinkle is back." The tips of Tristan's fingers grazed over it. "I don't like that."

"What *do* you like?"

"Well," Tristan said, and he was smiling again, his eyes that glowing, unearthly blue. Wade had been sure he must've done something electronic to enhance them in all his pictures, but here he was, his face an inch away from Wade's, and they were just as beautiful. "I did like this, before you stopped." He gave an experimental thrust of his own, and Wade couldn't help the groan that escaped out of his mouth. "But I think I'd like this even more."

Suddenly, Tristan's hand was on his hip and then his cock, a brief, glorious pressure that was gone way too soon. But this time when he dipped low, kissing Wade square on the mouth, the immediate pressure that Wade felt wasn't the curve of Tristan's hip but the curve of . . .

"Oh, God," he exhaled into Tristan's mouth. Pleasure was already rocketing through him as Tristan rocked down on him, and when he reciprocated, it blossomed, exponential and all-encompassing.

Surely he'd done this before, maybe not with a man, but with women? He'd had sex before. He wasn't a blushing virgin, but it had never felt like this.

He'd never felt like if he didn't see this through, if he didn't come his brains out, he'd regret it forever.

Hopefully Tristan was on board with that plan—and it seemed he was, because as hot as their kisses were, wet and searing, the way Tristan thrust against him was just as insistent.

Wade's hand circled Tristan's hip, encouraging him, and then slipped lower, right under the hem of his t-shirt, tracing surprisingly soft skin, and then went lower still.

He was firmly convinced that the curve of Tristan's ass could make grown men cry, and he'd only ever seen it. Touching it? A goddamn religious experience.

And the low groan that Wade felt rather than heard Tristan make? Even fucking hotter, if that was even possible.

Maybe dry humping each other until they exploded wasn't particularly high on the finesse charts, but right now, it was the sexiest sex act in the world to Wade, and he'd have fought anyone who claimed otherwise.

But there was no time for fighting, or for anything else, because Tristan's hands were all over, on his shoulders and his back and his hair, catching at the short hairs there, and he was moaning, and it all felt so goddamned amazing that Wade discovered that he couldn't hold back another second.

Tristan was panting, from exertion or pleasure, Wade wasn't sure, but he kissed him anyway, feeling his cock twitch and spurt in his shorts, riding the knife edge of pleasure. A second later, Tristan tensed, but didn't let go, and Wade let him work himself through it.

That, Wade realized in a daze as he started to come down from the endorphin high to realize his shorts were full of come, was the first orgasm he'd ever shared with another man.

If he'd known it would be that good, he'd have done this ages ago.

Of course, there'd never been anyone he'd ever wanted the way he wanted Tristan.

Maybe it was *just* Tristan.

This quixotic, unsurprisingly funny, surprisingly kind man.

"I think," Tristan finally said, not moving yet, "I might've banished that frown away forever."

"I think you well obliterated it," Wade said with a low, dry chuckle. "That was . . ."

"Fucking amazing?" It was Tristan's turn to laugh. "I wouldn't come in my pants for just anyone, you know."

"Speaking of that . . . we should get cleaned up."

"Good news is that I already thought of that." Tristan stood up on wobbly legs, and even though he could feel the stickiness seeping into his skin, into the fabric of his shorts, Wade nearly grabbed him and hauled him right back where he was.

His fingers itched with the desire to do it, even though he pushed the thought away even as Tristan's words began to sink in.

"You planned this?" Wade watched as Tristan rummaged around in one of the dresser drawers and came up with a pack of disposable cleaning cloths.

"Well, not exactly," Tristan said with a crooked smile, dropping his pants with very little fanfare and grabbing a cloth from the pack. "But I thought they might come in handy, no matter what."

Wade stood up and waddled over, picking his own from the pack. It was already damp and worked surprisingly well to clean up.

"A trick," Tristan said, pulling out fresh underwear, "from me to you. Free of charge."

"What was that orgasm, then?" Wade teased.

"Hopefully something we can repeat every night. Unless you're too tired, or you know, too sore . . ."

Wade rolled his eyes. "Don't you worry about me. I'm in the best shape of my life."

"Yeah, yeah, you really are," Tristan said, his gaze following each bit of Wade's exposed body. "It's a privilege, honestly."

"Glad you're enjoying it," Wade said. Meaning every word out of his mouth.

A fucking privilege, when it was Tristan Nicholson he was getting to touch. Wade wasn't good with words, or else he might be able to express just how much that meant to him.

How deep he was getting.

Because that was what was happening. Wade could feel it, even though he didn't quite know how to stop it.

He didn't want this to be just a fond memory he pulled out, of a few fun nights he and Tristan shared at camp.

He wanted it to be something he enjoyed every single fucking night.

That was alternatively terrifying and also wonderful.

Especially because he had no idea if Tristan felt the same way. Maybe this was something Tristan did all the time, hooked up with random guys, and then moved on. Maybe that was something that all queer guys did.

Wade didn't know, and found he was afraid to ask.

What if he didn't like the answer?

What if, even worse, Tristan didn't like the question?

What if it ruined this, which had turned out to be such a fucking amazing thing?

"I'm gonna go get ready for bed. We should turn in," Tristan said casually. "Early morning tomorrow."

It would be.

Even though it was stupidity to even consider it, Wade discovered that what he really wanted was to stay up and have Tristan pressed up against him, just talking. Just listening to his voice, and watching the light in his eyes. That's all.

But Tristan was already moving towards the bathroom, dressed only in a pair of briefs and a fresh t-shirt, so he could brush his teeth and wash his face.

Wade took the hint and put his pajamas on and followed suit.

But the whole time he was thinking, I want more nights. I want all the nights.

Tristan was sweating and just about to painfully pull himself upright, abs aching from another session with the dreaded medicine ball, when a hand he didn't recognize appeared in front of him.

He grasped it, the arm moving effortlessly to lift him up. Wiping the sweat from his eyes with a towel, Tristan nearly dropped it when he realized just who had helped him.

"Yo," Sebastian Howard said, "you must be new meat."

Tristan grinned. "You too, I hear."

"Nah," Sebastian said, with a wild grin, "you can only be new meat *once*. I'm just new to the team, that's all." He stretched out his hand again, and Tristan shook it, impressed by the confidence and strength in it, but not particularly surprised.

Sebastian Howard was pure energy and light contained in a six-foot-four-inch muscular frame, his huge brown arms covered in intricate swirling tattoos and his smile bright enough to light half of Florida.

"It's really nice to meet you, I'm . . ."

"Tristan Nicholson," Sebastian said, letting go of his hand. "I knew I recognized you from somewhere." He laughed. "All those PSAs."

Sometimes when people gave him shit about the series of advertisements he'd done for GLAAD, he felt a little bit embarrassed. Why had they picked him, when they could've picked so many more famous football players? Sam Crawford? Or Spencer Evans? Or even the O.G. of out football players, Colin O'Connor?

But they hadn't. They'd wanted someone young and hungry.

And, Tristan could practically hear Wade's wry, amused tone saying, *and 'cause you're hot, you idiot.*

Okay, maybe he didn't hate the way he looked when he looked in the mirror. And there were just extra bonus points when a really hot guy like Wade looked back, and then *kept* looking, even after they hung out.

"They were definitely everywhere," Tristan agreed, laughing.

"Couldn't throw a rock and not see you tossing a ball around and talking about how it gets better," Sebastian teased, but there was something blessedly non-judgmental about him that Tristan liked immediately.

"How can I say it doesn't, when it does?" Tristan dished right back.

"So true, so true," Sebastian said with a solemn nod.

Tristan had heard a rumor about Sebastian hooking up with a friend of a friend once—but he was pretty sure he wasn't out publicly. If that rumor had even been true.

It could've been the guy just bragging.

Tristan wouldn't have put it past that particular guy completely fabricating the entire event.

"Nobody giving you a hard time, then?" Sebastian asked.

Tristan grabbed his water bottle and took a long drink, trying to figure out what exactly Howard was getting at. "Uh, no?" he said.

"Unless you're counting Niko over there, because I'm convinced he's a sadist."

Sebastian laughed, and Tristan was one hundred percent not surprised to see the entire weight room turn in his direction.

There was something so alive and vital about Sebastian. Like he was lit from the inside.

Tristan was crushing hard on Wade, and he still couldn't quite tear his eyes away.

"Good," Sebastian said, patting him on the shoulder. "We gotta keep it that way, okay? So if you hear anything . . ."

Tristan took a risk.

"You mean, about a guy, I'd say about five foot nine, blond hair, green eyes, named Chris . . ."

Sebastian had been turning around, ready to head to the next lifting station when he wheeled back around. "You playin' games, aren't you, Nicholson?"

"Sure am, Howard."

Sebastian began to laugh. "Yeah, yeah, okay, but it's on the down low, you know? I ain't ready to share with the world yet. The team? I could give a shit, but the rest of everybody doesn't need to know."

"They don't ever have to," Tristan said honestly.

"Well, maybe someday, if I ever meet anyone worth sharin' for," Sebastian said with a suddenly easy grin. "And your friend Chris wasn't it, sad to say."

"Not my friend," Tristan retorted. "An . . . we'll call him an acquaintance." Tristan wasn't going to admit that he'd hooked up with him too. Had only found out about Chris' life goal of sleeping with as many football players as he could *after* the fact. And that, more than anything else, had essentially eliminated Chris' chances for a repeat.

Tristan had a feeling Sebastian had felt similarly about it.

Nobody wanted to be fucked for their cute hair or their pretty eyes or because they were really good at catching a ball.

"Huh, well, we'll say *past* acquaintance," Sebastian teased. He turned to go again, but called back over his shoulder, "Call me Sea Bass and I'm gonna call you Flounder, 'cause I intend to catch you all camp long."

"You can try," Tristan said. But had every intention of leaving Sea Bass' ass in the dust at their next practice.

He'd known of course, that there'd be veterans coming into camp. Paxton was already here, working out in the far corner with Davis hovering over him as he ran reps on the quad machine. But wow, Sebastian Howard guarding *him*. That was going to be freaking wild.

And a hell of a lot of fun.

"Who was that?"

Tristan turned and Wade was standing there, that same frown appearing between his brows.

Was he worried?

Or was he something else?

Suddenly Tristan wasn't sure.

Surely, Wade wouldn't be *jealous* of Sebastian Howard.

Surely.

"I thought we took care of this last night," Tristan said under his breath, pressing his fingertips against the crease between Wade's eyebrows.

Tristan knew men who paid thousands of dollars to get hair that incredible shade of burnished gold, and yet for Wade, it came as naturally as breathing.

"We did," Wade said, and his frown lightened, but it didn't go away completely.

"That was Sebastian Howard," Tristan said, because he wasn't quite as convinced as he'd been thirty seconds ago that Wade wasn't jealous. "You know, the shutdown corner the Piranhas signed in the offseason?"

"That was Sebastian Howard?" The crinkle deepened again.

"Sea Bass in person," Tristan said. "I didn't recognize him either."

"I think he shaved off his locs." Wade turned his head, and yeah, that was it, Tristan realized, following Wade's gaze to where Sebastian stood.

His locs had been incredible, long and luxurious, with a cool mix of his natural dark hair with a shocking white blond. But with them gone, you could really see his face, and it was an interesting, fascinating face, with a jawline that could cut glass.

"I think," Tristan said, lowering his voice, "that he's queer. And . . . well, I think he might have just confirmed it."

Wade looked shocked.

"Hey," Tristan said reprovingly, "I bet nobody thinks *you're* bi, either."

Wade choked on his water.

"Yeah, that's true," he admitted. "But wow, Sebastian Howard."

"There's more of us than anyone realizes, even though there are more and more guys being honest about their sexuality every year. Someone is always afraid it's gonna sink their NFL chances."

"Didn't you ever worry about that?" Wade *sounded* worried, still.

Tristan couldn't blame him. Not all of them were Heath Harris and Sam Crawford—they didn't even *need* to be.

Sometimes it was just about the freedom to live openly, without the terror of being discovered.

"All the time," Tristan admitted as he pushed open the door to the weight room. It was time for lunch, and the break couldn't come soon enough. "And then sometimes we do something to make it easier on others, and on ourselves, and *that* ends up hurting us."

"You don't mean all that great work you do on social media," Wade said, his voice disbelieving. "That *couldn't* hurt you."

"Tell that to my agent, *and* all those fucking sports media idiots, who claimed that my notoriety made it tougher to draft me."

"You said it better than I could: they're idiots." Wade's voice was very final and he sounded *and* looked just about ready to rip some arms from bodies. Tristan's heart grew a little warmer and he couldn't help but think that you really wouldn't want to piss Wade Lewis off—but that he was undeniably glad that Wade Lewis was pissed off on *his* behalf.

"Nobody ever said life was fair. Admittedly, next to those PSAs, I do like posting thirst traps," Tristan said, as they approached the buffet line.

"Thirst traps?" Wade looked confused.

Tristan laughed. "Sometimes I forget we're pretty different."

"Personally," Wade said as he grabbed a large bowl of lettuce, "I forget about it all the goddamned time."

Two days later, the rest of the veterans had reported to camp, and the situation and the schedule, Tristan had to admit, were more difficult than he'd imagined.

With the rest of the veterans reporting had come half a dozen more tight ends—the one veteran Piranhas player who'd been on the roster for a few years, plus a handful of others who'd been around, jumping from team to team, hoping to make a final roster someplace.

Wade was better, and had a ton of upside, but the existence of his competition stressed him out.

As for Tristan, all the competition did was make him want to win even more.

He was faster and quicker and frankly *smarter* than a lot of these guys, most of whom had spent their entire career riding a bench, and he had zero intention of letting any of them steal *his* roster spot.

It meant that for now, they fell into bed exhausted and overwhelmed, unable to do more than kiss goodnight.

It was disappointing, but Tristan decided, as he tried to limber up for the day's first practice, not really all that surprising.

Whatever was happening between him and Wade had always been a complete distraction as well as a waste of precious time and energy.

But tomorrow, they'd have a day off, and maybe . . . just maybe . . . he could convince Wade that it was high time they touched each other's dicks.

A lot.

But for now, they had to make it through this practice, an afternoon of meetings and film study, and then *another* more high-intensity practice, followed by yet another meeting.

And then . . . *finally* a day off.

"Let's huddle up," Pax said, leaning over, dark eyes intense, after they finished their warmup.

To Tristan's left was Kenyon Ellis, the Piranhas' starting running back, and on the other side of him, Carter Johnson, considered the best veteran wide receiver on the team, and then Wade, opposite him, flanked by the left tackle, Rob Jeremiah, and a few of the other linemen, including Logan Banks, the second-best center in the NFL.

First best was, of course, Brandon Phillips, who played for the Los Angeles Riptide. He'd refused to leave LA, but the Piranhas had thrown a bunch of money at Logan to convince him to leave Minnesota. And frankly, it probably hadn't taken much persuasion to leave snowy Minneapolis for sun-drenched Miami.

Paxton called the play, a deep fade right for Tristan, with a possible out for Wade, curling into the inside, just inside the first-down marker.

Tristan ignored the thrill of success already crashing through him at the thought of potentially getting the first catch of the practice, and instead focused, because *yeah*, that was definitely Sebastian Howard lining up opposite him.

Great. He was going to get pressed, first play of the day, in the first *practice* of the day, by Sea Bass himself.

He braced himself at the line of scrimmage, muscles tensed, head cocked to the right as Pax counted down, and then Rob snapped the ball. The second the ball left Rob's hands, Tristan exploded, running right past Sebastian. He chanced a look back when he was a good fifteen yards past the line of scrimmage, but

Sea Bass was holding strong, only a few steps behind, and gaining, running a very solid route behind him.

Shit, Tristan thought as Sebastian gained yet another step on him as they reached the twenty, and then thirty yards deep. The route Pax had called for Tristan to run button-hooked around the forty-yard line, and he began to shift his weight, to curl around, but Sebastian was right there, in his face.

Predictable route, Tristan could hear Pax saying in his head, *you ran it way too predictable. I'm gonna be lucky if I can throw this ball and Sea Bass doesn't just pluck it out of the air before you even have a chance of catching it.*

Tristan was not used to corners keeping up with him. In college, he'd blown right by most of them, almost nobody had managed to keep up with his unreal speed, but this, like Paxton had told him a few months back, was the NFL, and even the corners were fast as hell.

And Sebastian Howard? Definitely had it.

He craned his neck back around, locating where Pax was standing, ball in his hand, weight on the back foot, as Tristan had noticed he liked to do right before he tossed it. He let it fly right as Tristan recognized it, and he adjusted again, shoving an elbow into Sebastian's side as he maneuvered around him at the last second.

The thing was, Tristan was not only fast, he was *quick*, in the way that younger players usually were. Howard was older, over thirty now, and his reflexes, while still extraordinary, weren't the reflexes of a twenty-two-year-old.

Tristan jumped up, and tried to pluck the ball out of the air, but at the last second, Sebastian made a key adjustment that he hadn't seen coming and suddenly, right before the ball reached his hands, a gloved fist shot out and knocked it away.

He fell to the ground, hitting it hard, snapping his teeth shut on his mouth guard, feeling the impact reverberate through his body.

And he didn't have the fucking ball.

Sea Bass had knocked it away.

Coach Randy blew the play dead, and Sebastian leaned over him, shoving a hand out for him. The same fucking hand that had denied him.

Tristan took it anyway, because his grandfather had drilled good sportsmanship into his veins, and Sebastian was a teammate. "Hey, tough luck there," Sebastian said as they jogged back to the huddle.

It wasn't tough luck. It was all skill.

Sebastian had had the edge on that play, and Tristan hadn't. He'd counter-moved too late, running a predictable route, and letting Sea Bass in, giving him the second he needed to bat the ball away.

He was going to have to learn how to run better routes.

"Good effort, good effort," Coach Randy said, clapping as they returned to the line of scrimmage. "Both of you. And don't think I didn't see that elbow, Nicholson. You got away with it because this is a practice, but in a game, they call that."

"No way," Sebastian said with a grin. "It was just a puny little jab. Hardly nothing at all."

Tristan made a face.

He didn't look at Pax, and he definitely didn't look at Wade.

Wade would have caught that pass, probably because he could've physically muscled Sebastian away from it.

But Tristan didn't have Wade's bulk or his strength.

"After practice is over," Coach Randy said, turning to Tristan, "let's go over some routes, okay?"

Tristan wanted to make another face, because being called out on his deficiencies in front of the entire offense wasn't fun. But he didn't, because he was supposed to be learning, right?

Maybe he could pick this up, still. Wade was convinced he could. Tristan just had to convince *himself* that he wasn't just fast, that he could have other talents too.

That he wasn't just a one-trick pony.

Pax called them back into the huddle, and Tristan dutifully nodded at Coach Randy, and then returned to the huddle, listening as Pax detailed another pass play.

To Tristan's surprise, it was the same play.

The surprise must have shown because Pax shot him a look. "You've got to learn somehow, right?" he said.

Tristan had heard rumors for years that nothing, not two-a-days in high school, not spring camp in college, *nothing*, was as brutal as preseason camp in the NFL. It had always just made sense.

Everyone got better as only the best players remained. Naturally, you'd have to work harder.

But nothing had prepared Tristan for the realities of having Sebastian Howard cover him, and *only* him, for an entire two-hour practice.

Then he stayed for another forty minutes with Coach Randy, running routes over and over, listening to him bark and yell.

He thought, *maybe*, he was better after it.

Maybe.

Or maybe he was just really fucking tired and sore and beat down.

That was also possible.

Chapter Five

WADE WOKE PAINFULLY AND abruptly when the sun streamed through the crack in the cheap vinyl pull-down blind.

He realized, after not knowing where he was for a split second, that he was still at South Orange, still at Piranhas training camp, and the reason that stupid cracked blind hadn't woken him up before was because he'd gotten up every morning before the sun had had a chance to rise.

Today, their first day off since they'd gotten here seven days earlier, was the first chance he'd had to sleep in, and now the fucking sunshine had just woken him up.

He rolled over and heard a vague groaning from the other bed.

"Tristan, you awake too?" Wade asked softly.

Tristan's response was another groan.

Both the practices yesterday had been brutal.

Coach Randy, who had seemed nice enough on first introduction, had proved to be a brutal but effective taskmaster.

He'd not exactly taken it easy on Wade—because in his opinion, Wade could be a lot faster, kinda like Tristan, which was never happening—and Tristan could run routes a lot more like Wade.

When Tristan had fallen into bed last night, completely and utterly exhausted from their longest day yet, he'd said, "It's too bad for Coach Randy that we can't merge into one person, then he might actually do something crazy, like crack a smile."

Wade had laughed—he hadn't been able to help himself—but it had *hurt*. Still, he'd laughed anyway, through the pain, because Tristan, even wiped out and defeated, still had the most infectious sense of humor.

"I think you must be awake," Wade said. "I would like to officially lodge a request to subject that crack in the blind to one of Coach Randy's more inventive practices."

There was a chuckle from the other bed, and then a, "Goddamn it, Lewis, don't make me laugh. Niko was especially masochistic with that damned medicine ball yesterday."

"Yeah, but think of the thirst traps you'll be able to post once you have Niko-approved abs."

The problem was that Wade didn't want Tristan posting any thirst traps.

Except if they were sent to him and only him.

He wasn't usually a possessive kind of guy, but he'd never met anyone like Tristan before, and all he wanted was more.

Wade didn't know how Tristan would feel about that, if he told him, so he hadn't.

Neither of them knew if they'd even be playing on the same team in a few weeks, so it made sense to keep it casual. That was logical; the problem was that Wade's heart was increasingly involved and hearts weren't very logical.

"Trust me," Tristan retorted dryly, "if I can barely dredge up the energy to kiss *you*, I'm not going to be posting any thirst traps anytime soon."

"Think about it, a *whole day off*, though," Wade said. He knew how excited he sounded.

"Is it really a day off if I can't move?" Tristan wondered from his side of the room.

"It's a day off even if you spend it in bed."

Which . . . Wade definitely wouldn't be complaining if that was how Tristan wanted to spend the day.

He heard a low chuckle from Tristan. "I know what's on *your* mind," he teased.

"I would absolutely tell Coach Randy he's a dirty cockblocker," Wade said, his pulse racing a little faster at even the *word* cock, "but then I'd have to tell him why, and he might not like that very much, and frankly, he already doesn't like us very much."

"Are you kidding, he fucking loves you," Tristan groaned. "You didn't have to run fifty routes yesterday."

"Oh, but I got to run *sprints* instead," Wade said.

Tristan laughed again, and gasped. "God, stop being so funny, okay? You're killing me."

"No, that's a little later . . ." Wade said slyly. Already thinking about it.

Okay, that was a lie.

He'd never stopped thinking about it.

"I'm gonna hold you to that," Tristan said, "when I'm not suffering so much over here."

"No complaints from this side."

"You're pretty eager for a newbie bi, with an Air Force general for a dad," Tristan said contemplatively.

"You're the one who taught me that none of those things are important," Wade said. He'd actually begun to believe it too.

It helped that nobody on the Piranhas seemed to give two shits what your sexuality was. They just wanted you to play "lights out" football, and to notch wins.

An attitude Wade could get behind.

"You're right, none of them are," Tristan said, his voice warm.

"Don't be so nice, or I might come over there," Wade faux-threatened.

Tristan groaned. "Not yet. I haven't worked out the hundred places on my body that really fucking hurt."

"Just a hundred?"

"You really don't get enough credit for being funny," Tristan said. "I never once heard any of those sports journalist assholes talk about how funny you were. Just how tall you were, how much you could bench, how high you could jump. I feel like you should sue."

"I should," Wade agreed, feeling a warmth spread out inside him.

Maybe he was in just as much pain as Tristan. Everything fucking ached.

But he wanted to do this every single morning forever.

Maybe in the same bed. That would be nice.

And without all the aching muscles, too.

"So, what are we doing today?" Tristan said. "We spending it in bed?"

"Not two separate beds," Wade said with a snort.

"Too bad they didn't consider our needs ahead of time and give us a nice queen or something."

"Imagine Beau's face if we told him that's what we needed," Wade guffawed, even though he wouldn't ever dare.

"I think he might be a little jealous," Tristan said.

"Is he single, then?" Wade wondered.

"I don't know, but I bet he is. We're all fucking married to the game, aren't we?"

I'm not, Wade thought, even though he knew he should be, *and I don't want you to be either.*

"He's never mentioned a boyfriend to me," Wade said.

"That's right," Tristan said, snapping his fingers. "You're all tight with him. From rookie camp."

"We're . . . we're not *close*," Wade protested. "He's a good guy. A . . . well, I guess I would call him a friend."

"What would you call me?" Tristan's voice was sly and teasing, and Wade wanted nothing more than to crawl out of bed and go over to Tristan's and kiss the sass right out of his mouth.

But that would mean moving, and it would be considerably less impressive if Wade collapsed to the ground only halfway to where Tristan lay.

Wade considered Tristan's question for a long second. He already knew he couldn't tell him the truth; he didn't know all the rules, at least not yet but even he wasn't naive enough to think the truth wouldn't scare the shit out of Tristan.

It definitely scared the shit out of Wade.

"A friend, with plenty of benefits," Wade finally said.

"Took you long enough. I think I can see the smoke coming out of your ears from all the way over here," Tristan teased.

"I was just thinkin' about all the benefits we haven't gotten to enjoy yet." That wasn't even a lie. He had been. How could he not when Tristan was just over there, all cute and warm and sleep-rumpled.

Wade wanted to rumple him up some more.

"So that's what you want to do today," Tristan stated, rather than asked, speculatively.

"Some of that, some relaxin', and maybe even going over some tape with Beau. He offered last night. Offered for you too. Wanted to show you some film of Sea Bass' past coverages. Give you a leg up for tomorrow."

"As long as I'm watching it and not running it," Tristan said.

"I can't believe you convinced me to do this, today of all days," Tristan groaned as they walked towards the section of the South Orange athletic complex that the Piranhas coaching staff had taken over for their temporary offices.

It turned out that Wade was crazy and he'd agreed to meet Beau at ten.

"On our freaking day off," Tristan had muttered under his breath as he'd slid, painfully, out of bed.

"You want to make Sea Bass and Coach Randy eat their words?" Wade had asked, even though Tristan knew he didn't need to really ask the question.

Of course he did.

He wanted to not only show both of them what he was capable of, but make the goddamned team.

If that meant dragging his sorry, worn-out ass to Beau's office instead of spending the morning in bed with Wade, he'd do it.

Because it might mean that he could spend *many* mornings in bed with Wade.

They hadn't discussed it. Tristan knew the benefits to keeping things casual, especially when their futures were so uncertain, but he couldn't deny what he wanted.

One, to make the team, and a very, very close second: Wade.

Even better, he wanted both, *together*.

He'd taken a sleepy selfie this morning—not precisely a thirst trap, but he'd been really pleased to see when he got out of the shower that Wade had already liked it.

They'd shared one hot kiss, with the promise of more later, before heading out for Beau's office.

Wade knocked on Beau's open door, and the coach's son looked up.

He was still wearing those ridiculous dark-rimmed glasses, like he was Clark freaking Kent and they'd prevent anyone from realizing how attractive he was.

He was no Wade Lewis, but it was, Tristan decided as they walked in and sat down opposite Beau, an undeniable fact that he was attractive.

If he knew Beau as well as Wade apparently did, he'd have teased him about trying to hide his beauty behind a bushel, but he didn't, not yet anyway.

And it would feel weird, Tristan decided, to tell someone in front of Wade that he thought they were attractive.

It was silly and it wouldn't mean anything, but the last thing Tristan wanted was for Wade to get the wrong idea.

Like all his bones didn't freaking melt in his body whenever he even so much as glanced in Wade's direction.

All the bones that is, except one.

"Hey, guys," Beau said, standing up at his desk and smiling at them. "Glad to see you."

"Even on our day off," Tristan joked.

"Day off? What's that?" Beau teased right back. "If you think the old man works *you* hard, imagine being related to him."

Tristan couldn't imagine it, because his dad had been a massive piece of shit.

But he imagined that Wade might feel something similar to Beau—might be why they'd bonded so easily—considering that his father was a general in the Air Force. Talk about overachieving.

"You ever consider working for someone else?" Wade wondered.

"Nope," Beau said, shaking his head. "Nowhere I'd rather be, to be honest. As crazy as that sounds. Now, I know you're interested in some historic coverages that Howard has run in the past, Tristan. You wanna start there?"

"Sure," Tristan said, pulling out his tablet.

"You might as well pay attention, Wade, 'cause I have a feeling once Tristan here has cracked Sea Bass' code, he's comin' after you next." Beau pulled up something on his own tablet, and then suddenly the video was up on the big-screen TV on the wall.

"Oh, I believe it," Wade said ruefully.

"Let's start with a game that the Giants played against the Seahawks last year," Beau said, and he circled Sebastian's position on his tablet, the same red markings showing up on the TV. "He got the unlucky assignment of covering DK Metcalf all game. They fought in the fucking trenches for four quarters, and even though Sea Bass has lost a step in the last few seasons, Metcalf didn't catch a single deep pass."

"Wait a second," Tristan said, "you think Sea Bass has *lost* a step?"

Beau grinned. "Still giving you a hard time, isn't he?"

"I think Howard might kill you for even daring to suggest he's not as fast or as good as he used to be."

"Oh, he's still as good, maybe even better, now that he's lost a step," Beau said, "because he's had to compensate for the loss of speed."

"He hasn't lost a goddamned step," Tristan muttered under his breath. Howard was giving him fucking fits, and Tristan definitely hadn't gotten any slower.

"I promise you, he has," Beau said solemnly. "It's my job to see it. He's found ways to compensate for it, but I guarantee that if you challenged him to running a straight forty, you'd blow him away."

"That's an idea," Wade said thoughtfully.

"No, it's not," Tristan said. "He's after me enough as it is."

"Yeah, well, here's where I can teach you his tricks," Beau said, jerking them back on subject. "This game against DK Metcalf, he employed all of them, trying to contain him."

Beau tapped the screen. "Here's the first one. He did this to you a lot yesterday, Tristan, so you should recognize it—using his height and his ability to reach a crazy altitude to knock the ball away."

"Yeah," Tristan said, trying not to sound testy. How many passes had Sebastian cost him with that little move? He didn't know, but it had been frustrating as hell. He'd thought he'd had the ball more than once, only to realize at the last second that Sea Bass had batted it away.

"I know you're asking yourself, how do you prevent him from being his freakish self? DK kept asking himself the same question the whole game. But he figured it out in the fourth quarter. Look at this," Beau said, starting the video. He'd slowed it down, so that both Howard and Metcalf moved a frame at a time, and it was easy to track them across the screen.

Metcalf made a sudden spin move, at the very end of the route, turning away from Howard at the last minute, and when Russell Wilson threw the ball, Metcalf had clearly warned him he was going to make the move, because they connected for a solid forty-yard gain.

No chance for Howard to knock the pass away.

"That's sweet," Tristan said, scribbling down notes onto his tablet. He wanted to practice that. He knew he'd basically been hobbling around only an hour before, but now he wanted to get back onto the practice field and try that. "That's almost like . . . almost a running back move, when they break through the defensive line."

"Yep," Beau said with a nod. "And it worked."

"I remember that play," Wade said. "I watched that game."

"Here's the thing, if you can best Howard, you can best most of the cornerbacks in this league," Beau said leaning forward and putting his elbows on the desk. "It's rough to practice against him now, but it's gonna give you an edge for later."

"You give him these kinds of compliments?" Wade asked.

"Nope." Beau was grinning. "I tell him he's lost a step."

Tristan could only imagine how well that went over. Anyone who played professional football had a healthy ego; Sebastian's ego was a little more than healthy. Of course with his legendary skills, it was also earned.

Tristan had learned that much, over the last few days of Sebastian covering him.

"Okay, got that spin move down? Let's go over some of the other tricks," Beau said.

For the next forty-five minutes, Beau went over some really great curated moments he'd found in Sea Bass' archives.

Tristan wasn't naive; he knew how much time it must have taken to find them and put them together.

When the session was over, and he and Wade were standing up to go, Tristan paused at the doorway. "Thanks, man," he said, really meaning it, "you totally saved my fucking bacon."

"Don't thank me," Beau said, "this is what Coach hired me to do. Find the shit that nobody else takes the time to find."

"You really a genius?"

"No," Beau said, chuckling under his breath, though at the same time Wade nodded.

"What?" Wade said. "Coach told me your IQ. You're a fucking genius, dude, don't try to deny it."

"You shouldn't," Tristan agreed. "And those glasses? Aren't fooling anyone for a second. You're still Superman."

Beau looked confused, and so Tristan was forced to explain.

Maybe he had a genius IQ but it seemed he hadn't taken much time over the years to keep up with comic book pop culture. Wade was probably right; he was totally married to the game.

"Clark Kent tried to disguise that he was freaking Superman with these glasses," Tristan said, "and it always worked, but it really shouldn't have."

"Well, I actually need these," Beau said ruefully. "Unfortunately. Contacts don't like my eyes much."

Tristan concluded he'd pushed his luck enough for one day and decided he wouldn't be telling the guy he'd be so much cuter without the big frames. "Well, thanks again," he said. "I really appreciate it."

They shook hands, and then Wade did his fun handshake with Beau again.

"Just torment the shit out of him tomorrow for me, okay?" Beau said.

"Can do," Tristan said, and for the first time since camp started, he thought he might really be able to pull this off.

At least if he kept Beau on his side.

Chapter Six

"So, let me get this straight," Wade said, and he heard the twang in his own voice. He wasn't really ashamed of it, except when he felt like he wasn't in on the joke. "You just . . . put this card out, on the green side, and they just . . . keep bringing you meat?"

But Tristan didn't make fun of him. He didn't laugh. He just grinned and said, "Great, isn't it?"

"Don't tell me you've never been to a Brazilian steakhouse before, Lewis," Sebastian teased—but he didn't sound particularly mean or judgmental.

"I hadn't been to one either, before some guys on the offensive line dragged me last year," Pax said kindly. "Made me pay for them to eat their own weight in meat, but you know, those guys protect my ass every week, so it was worth it."

"There's also the salad bar," Logan added, "for those of us who might want to eat something green."

"Something green? You're gonna waste stomach room on something *green*?" Sebastian laughed. "No, thank you, I'm eating all the meat in the world. *All* the meat."

"Nobody is surprised by this," Logan said, deadpan.

Wade didn't know Logan all that well, though he wanted to. But they hadn't had many times to talk, even in a group, and he was hoping, because they'd both ended up coming out tonight, that he could change that.

The man was quiet, but he had a disarming and dry sense of humor that had caused Wade to laugh out loud more than once when they'd been at practice.

Wade reached out and flipped over the green card. "And that's all I have to do?" he asked again.

"Yep," Tristan said. "I'm gonna go check out the salad bar with Logan. Anyone else want to join?"

Wade usually never wanted to go anywhere without Tristan, but he was just fine *not* loading up on salad. He shook his head, but the two of them headed off.

"Thanks for inviting some of us rookies," Wade said to Sebastian.

Sea Bass, as Tristan had told him he liked to be called, leaned back in his chair. "Someone's gotta take the rookies under their wing. I figured why not me."

But Wade could hear the seriousness in his voice. "I suppose we should thank you for running us ragged during the week."

"Nope, no football talk," Sebastian said. "None whatsoever. We haven't had a single conversation about anything that *wasn't* football for seven days, and I'm done."

"Okay . . ." Wade hesitated. What were they supposed to talk about?

"How about, you and Tristan seem like you're growing closer," Pax said, leaning forward, an engaging smile on his face.

"Uh," Wade said. They hadn't talked about telling anyone yet. Were they so obvious that everyone had figured it out on their own? God, he hoped not. He didn't want to scare Tristan away. He was less concerned that this team wouldn't accept him if they knew he was queer. After all, they'd accepted Tristan, who was as open as they came.

"He's a good guy. Sweeter than you'd imagine, from his Instagram feed. Cares about people."

That was safe enough, Wade decided.

"That's true," Pax said thoughtfully. "I'd have guessed he was pretty full of himself. But he isn't."

"Not at all," Wade said. Didn't feel like it was right to confess that Tristan wasn't nearly as confident as he pretended when he was in front of the camera.

Tristan had been honest and vulnerable to him; but that didn't mean he was ready to be that way with these other guys.

"I ended up rooming with some insane guy my rookie year," Paxton observed, after the first set of waiters had come around with their gigantic skewers of meat, slicing off huge chunks for the three of them.

"I think we all have some kind of horror story from our rookie year," Sebastian agreed. "And I'll allow those, 'cause most of the time they aren't actually because of football, right, Pax?"

Paxton nodded as he cut into his meat. "This guy liked to snort protein powder. But the doctor told him to quit it, because it was really dangerous—and he wasn't wrong. So instead of doing that, he started shoving it up his ass. In *front* of me."

"Ew," Logan said as he and Tristan returned to the table. "What are you talking about, Pax?"

"My old roommate last year. The one who'd just strip down, and . . . *you know.*"

"You should've just told him to put his ass away," Sebastian said.

"Yeah, not a good look when I was trying to prove how tough I was," Pax said with a beleaguered sigh. "I put up with it. And what, the guy didn't even make the team."

"He'd probably shredded all his brain cells before the doctor got him to stop," Wade said.

"Believe me, that was not what I expected someone was shoving up someone's ass," Tristan teased.

"Oh, what you thinkin' of, Flounder?" Sebastian asked.

Tristan flushed. "Just saying, I was not expecting the story to end that way, when it started . . . well, when it started like that."

"You got any horror stories from your rookie year, Logan?" Pax asked. "Other than someone convincing you that you need to eat salad when you come to a Brazilian steakhouse?"

"Balance is important," Logan said with a dignity that Wade couldn't help but respect. "And yeah, of course, we all do, right?"

"Well, I don't. Not yet, anyway," Tristan said, and Wade felt his hand reach out and squeeze his knee, under the coverage of the table.

"Maybe we'll get lucky," Wade offered.

The extra gleam in Tristan's blue eyes suggested he'd like to get lucky *a lot*. Wade was totally on board with that plan.

"Yeah, you've never come in the room and your roommate's naked? That could be a fun kind of lucky," Sebastian teased.

Wade was suddenly sure that Sebastian knew, but how could he? They had to just be assuming. Or guessing.

But a quick look over at Tristan made it clear that he wasn't concerned at all. So Wade let it go and took another bite of sirloin, which was absolutely delicious.

"My story isn't that kind of fun, at all," Logan said, and okay, maybe they hadn't been invited because they were rookies . . . but because of something else. Tristan had said he was pretty sure Sebastian was queer. And now Logan with saying that was *fun*, then . . . maybe he was too. He hadn't heard any rumors about Pax, but maybe . . .

There couldn't be any about him, Wade was sure of it. He'd been in the league only a few months. But maybe they'd invited him because he was Tristan's roommate and they didn't want to leave him out.

That's, he told himself, what it *had* to be.

"What kind of fun *is* it?" Sebastian asked, a sly smile on his face.

"Oh, your regular uber-competitive kind of fun. The guy was another lineman. He'd played several different spots on the line in college, and the Vikings did it differently than the Piranhas do. They encourage a lot of competition, thinks it makes everyone a better player. So they pushed, and he pushed, just way too far, never a moment of peace, and so halfway through camp, I stole all his cups."

The whole table laughed. Sebastian literally *cackled*.

"What did he do?" Tristan wanted to know.

"Oh, he could've gone to the equipment manager," Logan said. "But he didn't, because he felt stupid, having to explain where they'd gone. So he played without them."

"Really?" Wade couldn't believe it.

Logan shrugged. "He was trying to prove he was the toughest guy out there. Guess he lost that bet. It's gonna be tough to explain to the future mother of his children why there won't *be* any."

"That's insanity," Pax said, shaking his head. "And toxic masculinity at work, too. There's plenty of that in the NFL, but that doesn't mean it's not fucked up."

"The most fucked up," Sebastian agreed.

And that, Wade decided, was the truth.

These guys didn't give a shit what made them men, or who decided if they were men or not, and that's what made them *great* men.

The not-giving-a-shit part. If he ended up like them, even a little bit, then he'd consider it a job well done.

And if he could play football next to them? Even better.

"It turns out that you weren't wrong, Beau *is* a genius," Tristan said as he pulled his t-shirt off.

After the steakhouse, they'd come back and watched a movie.

The guys had put another movie on, but Tristan hadn't had to fake his yawns when he'd claimed he was tired and headed back to the room and nobody had questioned when Wade had stood up too, going with him.

Transitioning from friends who hung out and teammates who helped each other to guys who wanted each other was still a tiny bit awkward. Tristan assumed it was probably easier for him than it was for Wade, who was still getting used to hooking up with a guy. But then Tristan had never hooked up with a teammate either.

He'd never liked one enough to counteract the inherent risk. And, oh, he liked Wade plenty. Liked him too much, if he was going to admit to the whole truth.

Could probably, terrifyingly, love him, if they kept doing this.

Tristan hadn't come to the Piranhas camp to fall in love but sometimes fate knew what you needed better than you did.

"Yeah, yeah, you keep sayin' that," Wade said as he shed his sweatpants. "Should I be jealous?"

Should Wade be jealous?

Absolutely fucking no.

"No way," Tristan said.

"I was just teasin'," Wade said lightly, but there was that furrow in his brow again. Tristan couldn't miss it.

Normally, they only made that final transition from friends to lovers when the lights went out. But tonight, Tristan threw caution to the wind and went over to Wade and wrapped his arms around him, pulling him close.

"Trust me, you've got nothing to worry about," he said. "I don't see anybody but you."

Wade sighed and melted into Tristan's embrace.

This was the problem.

Not the only problem by a long shot, but definitely the *biggest* problem. Tristan already knew he cared more than he should, and unless he was totally wrong, Wade was right there with him. Inevitably, this was going to be more than some hot and heavy hookup at camp—unless fate decided to fuck with them some more, and one of them didn't make the team—but Tristan still didn't know what to do about it.

Sure, Coach Dawson was okay with Beau being gay and working for him, but how would he feel if he discovered that two of his rookie players were hooking up?

Tristan felt a shiver of anxiety move through him.

"I think," Wade said softly, "that's your crinkle."

"My crinkle?" Tristan questioned, even though he knew exactly what Wade was talking about.

"You kind of tremble every once in awhile, when it's too much," Wade said. "Like how I frown, right between my eyebrows. That crinkle you wish you could get rid of. I wish I could get rid of your tremor."

So much for Wade not seeing him.

He had a feeling that Wade saw all of him.

Tristan tilted his head up and pressed his lips to Wade's. Soft, but it didn't take long for the kiss to heat up. That was the thing about Wade; even when Tristan was exhausted and sore and stressed, he still wanted him all the time.

Even when he knew it would be way better not to want him at all.

"God," Wade exhaled on a groan as Tristan moved his mouth across his scruffy neck and ended up at his earlobe, nibbling with some definite force.

Wade might end up with teeth marks on his ear tomorrow.

He liked the idea of marking Wade as all his.

"Like that?" Tristan asked. He already knew, because Wade's hips were already moving, like he couldn't even help it, and his cock was hard and hot against Tristan's thigh. But sometimes it was nice to hear Wade *say* it.

"God, I fucking love it," Wade said between moans.

His hands were everywhere, on Tristan's face, sliding down from his neck to his back and then lower still, gripping first his ass, and then his hips. He felt the drumbeat pulse in his own cock, heady and quick, and he felt like one enormous nerve, everywhere Wade touching him lighting him up.

"You wanna try something different?"

Tristan would be happy—he'd be fucking *thrilled*—to just make out and dry hump Wade forever. But he'd yet to get up close and personal with the dick currently rubbing against him, and he wanted to see it. He wanted to touch it. He wanted to taste it.

Maybe that might be a lot for Wade, but Tristan reasoned that he'd been nothing but burning enthusiasm so far, so maybe he might be open to moving things along in a more physical direction.

"Anything," Wade said, and the look in those unearthly gray eyes was full of truth.

Tristan reached down and tugged his t-shirt up, enjoying the sight of Wade's uncovered chest, bulging with muscle, the trail of brown hair leading to his shorts.

He stroked it, because he couldn't help himself. Wanted to touch lower. But made sure to glance up at Wade's face as he nudged him closer to the bed. Wanted to make sure that he wasn't doing anything Wade wasn't a hundred and ten percent on board with.

But Wade's gaze was excited and eager, and when the back of his knees hit the edge of the bed, he went down easily. It was even easier for Tristan to tuck himself in between those incredible muscular thighs, every inch he wanted to bite and lick, leave his mark behind.

He couldn't. Not now.

But he let his mind wander, imagining a future in which he could brand Wade as only his.

Where nobody would blink twice at the idea that Wade Lewis and Tristan Nicholson were fucking.

Fucking and maybe even more.

"You're . . ." Wade's face, as he looked down at Tristan, was worshipful.

"I'm what?" Tristan teased as his fingers tucked under Wade's shorts and began to tug them down.

"You're fucking incredible," Wade said. "But I bet all the boys who let you between their legs say that."

"Not as many as you might think," Tristan said.

He was, despite the way his social media habits made him look, picky.

He didn't do this all the time.

He didn't even want to.

But with Wade? His mouth was fucking watering.

Even more when he got Wade's shorts down and he realized that Wade had managed to hide from him in the locker room one important fact: that he'd neglected to put anything under the shorts.

Wade's cock bobbed out, hard and heavy, flushed red at the tip, and Tristan couldn't help it. Leaning forward, he gave the head an experimental lick.

Wade groaned loud.

Way too loud.

"You gotta be quiet," Tristan hissed.

"Shit, I don't know how I can be," Wade said honestly, digging his fingertips into his bedding.

"You gotta," Tristan said.

Wade gave him a sharp nod.

And then Tristan couldn't wait a moment longer. He leaned in again and this time took in a few inches, curling his tongue around the head, tasting that particular woody scent of Wade for the first time.

"Fuck." Wade's exhaled curse was quieter this time, but had a devastating edge to it. "Not gonna . . ."

Tristan didn't expect that he would last long. He was pretty good at sucking cock, despite the pickiness, and he had a feeling that Wade hadn't had anything really good like this in . . . well, *ever*.

And he intended to make it good. So good that Wade wouldn't ever forget it, no matter what happened in a few weeks.

No matter what happened tomorrow.

He let another few inches slip into his mouth, and sucked hard, loving the way Wade jolted and swore again, under his breath. Loved the strain on Wade's handsome face, the way his eyes screwed shut.

Decided he was going to wring every ounce of surprised pleasure out of the man.

It wasn't so hard to readjust his angle slightly, and cup his balls with his other hand, pulling them slightly, just as he dipped his head even lower.

Wade was big, and it was a lot to take, but Tristan breathed through it, and Wade's electrified reaction was worth every bit of discomfort.

He let Wade's cock slip out of his lips, spit-slick and iron-hard, and then he took him deep again, and then again, until Wade was straining above him, face a pleasured grimace.

Meanwhile he babbled the whole time in a thick Texas accent about how good it was, how much he liked Tristan, how sexy he was, how good HE was, that had Tristan hard as a fucking rock, maybe the hardest he'd ever been in his whole goddamn life.

He could've kept going forever, just like this, the praise of the man he was crushing so hard on falling onto his head like snowflakes, his cock hard and heavy in his mouth, but too soon, Wade began to thrash around a little and his voice shifted, and Tristan knew he was close.

He took him deep again, felt him shudder and flex, and sucked him right through it, swallowing every bit of come.

It took a good minute for Wade to stop twitching, and only then did Tristan slip his softening cock out of his mouth.

"Holy fuck," Wade said with a sharp exhale.

Tristan's own dick was so hard, he could feel each pulse of his heartbeat.

He didn't want to rush Wade. Wanted him to enjoy the afterglow.

But goddamn it, he was going to need *something* soon.

"Come 'ere," Wade said then, suddenly, and very unexpectedly.

"What?" There wasn't much blood left in Tristan's brain; that was his only excuse.

"You just about blew my brain right off," Wade said, and Tristan was surprised at how much he liked this praise thing. "I can't claim I can do the same thing. Yet, anyway. But I can . . ." Tristan watched as he swallowed hard, his Adam's apple bobbing. "I can still make you feel good."

"Yeah?"

"Yeah." Wade sounded very confident.

There was nothing sexier on earth than a confident Wade Lewis.

Tristan let him pull his t-shirt off, then his shorts, and then his big, rough, calloused hand was closing around his own dick, the other curled around his hip, and he was still goddamned talking.

"Oh yeah, just like that," Wade cooed, "I'm gonna make you feel so good, you're gonna come so hard, right like that, just like that . . ."

Tristan might have had the more experience between the two of them, but embarrassingly only a little bit of Wade sex-talking him through a handjob was apparently enough to make him lose it completely.

His orgasm shorted out his own brain, and he might have yelped.

Okay, he definitely yelped as he came and came into Wade's hand and he pumped him right through it.

It might not have been the best handjob he'd ever received, but somehow it was heads and tails above every other sexual encounter he'd ever experienced.

Just because it was Wade.

And it was Wade kissing him as he came down from the endorphin rush of it. And Wade cuddling him on the bed after he'd cleaned up his hand.

"I wish," Wade said into the quiet, "that we didn't have to . . . well, you know."

"Didn't have to what?"

"This separate-bed bullshit." Wade's voice was hushed. "I like cuddling with you."

Tristan liked cuddling with him too, and he'd never cared one way or the other about it before. But with Wade it was like he couldn't quite bear to let him go.

"I like it too," Tristan admitted, even though he knew it was a bad idea to be so honest.

Because where was this honesty going to get them? He didn't know. But he felt closer to Wade than any other guy he'd been with. Was it because they'd become friends too? Because they'd been through the hell of camp together?

Or was it something else, something so much more enduring? Something lasting?

Tristan was afraid it was totally developing into the latter.

"We could always just take the mattresses off the beds," Wade said in that contemplative tone of voice that Tristan had already discovered didn't always bode well.

"And what? Shove them together?"

"I don't want to sleep without you," Wade said stubbornly. He glanced down at Tristan, and there was that emotion again in his eyes.

An emotion that Tristan felt echoed inside of him, too, and that he was still terrified to name.

You couldn't fall in love with someone in less than a week.

He didn't *want* to fall in love with anyone.

Not when football was supposed to be his new boyfriend.

Except he had a feeling that ship had already sailed.

"I don't want to sleep without you either," Tristan said, and he was already moving away from Wade, with the enticing promise of them sleeping together—just sleeping, he couldn't quite believe it himself—beckoning. "We'll just have to move them back every morning. Not like we don't normally get up at the ass crack of dawn anyway."

"Exactly," Wade said, and he was grinning infectiously. "Come on, get your cute butt in gear."

And Tristan tumbled the rest of the way, head over heels, in love with him.

Chapter Seven

The next morning, Wade didn't wake up slowly, but suddenly, a loud thumping echoing through his ears.

He also woke on the floor, with Tristan starfished over him, like he was Wade's favorite new blanket.

And, Wade realized as his brain began to function, he was.

They were going to have to do something about this.

It was completely and totally unexpected, but he wasn't going to let Tristan go, no matter how crazy it seemed to pursue a relationship with him right now.

He was feeling things he'd never felt before, and that wasn't even counting the way that Tristan had sucked every coherent thought he'd ever had right out of his head.

There was something deeper going on here.

Something that made Wade believe other forces had to be at work. But even if them meeting here was fate, he wasn't going to leave anything up to chance.

They were going to have to work harder than they'd ever worked in their life to guarantee they both made the Piranhas' final roster and that football, which had brought them together, didn't end up separating them.

The pounding continued, and Wade thought, for a single second, about dislodging Tristan and going to see what the big ruckus was, but then he thought, *naw, too much effort*. And besides, he was nice and toasty warm right here, with the guy he was falling for, draped across him. *Besides*, Wade reasoned, *we locked the door, right?*

Wade realized a second too late, that no, they hadn't, and he wasn't just a little bit wrong, he was a *lot* wrong.

The door opened and Tristan's eyes flew open and they both looked up guiltily into the eyes of Beau Dawson.

"Uh," Tristan said eloquently, and Wade couldn't do anything else. He laughed.

Beau looked mighty surprised, and also a little bit embarrassed.

"Oh, shit, sorry, I didn't . . ." He fumbled. "I didn't expect . . ."

Wade was still laughing as Tristan leveraged himself up. Thank God they'd both had a single thought in their heads after those fucking fantastic orgasms and they'd both put underwear back on. Or else Beau would've gotten an eyeful too.

Maybe, though, it would've been better to have *two* thoughts in their head, Wade considered, and they'd have remembered to lock the door.

"Why would you?" Tristan said dryly. "Because this would be crazy."

"A little," Beau said sheepishly, rubbing his neck, not quite sure where to look, that much was obvious.

Tristan was pulling a t-shirt on, but Wade could still see that delectable curve of his ass peeking out from under it and it was almost enough to distract him.

Almost.

"Well, I guess the cat's out of the bag," Wade said, standing up with a groan.

"Wait, this is a thing? Not just a . . ." Beau looked a little lost.

Wade glanced over at Tristan, who was looking right back. He shrugged. "It's something," he said. "We haven't exactly had a chance to talk about it yet."

"Is the something a distraction?" Beau asked.

"No," Tristan said resolutely. "No, not even remotely. In fact, I'd argue that we make each other better football players."

"And we both want this so bad, so we're gonna work harder than anyone else," Wade added.

Beau chuckled under his breath. "You know this is nuts, right?"

"Yep, we know," Wade said. "But sometimes . . . well, you know how it is."

"No, I don't know," Beau said dryly. "But . . . listen, I don't want to be the guy who rats you out to my dad. I think you've got real potential to make this team. You're both bringing something hot to the table, and not just . . ." He waved between them awkwardly. "Whatever this is. I want to see you guys develop it. So, I'm not going to say anything."

"Thank you, you are a fucking lifesaver," Tristan said.

"Yet," Beau concluded with finality. "I'm not going to say something *yet*. But when the time comes and you both make the team—which I will still, I might add, help you do—you'd better come clean with him. He deserves to know."

"What if that . . ." Tristan didn't finish the sentence but the apprehension in his eyes spoke volumes.

"If he likes you, he likes you. I guarantee you he does not give a single shit where you put your dick when you're off his football field." Beau's words were succinct and rang with honesty. "And speaking of football fields, that's why I came by. I thought you might want to put a little early morning work in, so get your butts in gear, okay?" He turned around and left, shutting the door behind him with a bit more force than was probably entirely necessary.

Wade burst into laughter the moment the door was closed.

"Are you fucking crazy?" Tristan said, looking at him like he thought he was. "We just got found out and you're *laughing* about it."

"Yeah, yeah," Wade said. "But you heard him. Coach doesn't give a shit. We just gotta make the team. Get dressed, sweetcheeks, we've got some plays to practice."

Tristan was still vibrating though, even as Wade went to his drawers to grab practice clothes. "What if . . ."

"Listen," Wade said, turning, and putting his hands on Tristan's face. "I care about you. Do you care about me?"

He didn't know what Tristan was going to say—he hoped the guy would be keeping him on his toes for years to come, if he was being completely honest with himself—but he found he wasn't nervous at all. He knew what this felt like, even if he'd never really experienced it before.

You didn't feel this way and feel this way alone.

"I do," Tristan said.

"Do you want to be with me?"

"I do," Tristan repeated, this time sticking his chin out defiantly. Like he was defying his own better judgement.

"Then, I don't see the problem." Wade turned back to the drawers.

"Wait," Tristan said, catching his shoulder. "You . . . you really want to do this? *This*? A relationship? With me?"

"I absolutely do," Wade said. "Not a doubt in my mind."

Tristan looked floored which made Wade pissed off at every other guy who hadn't really given a shit about him. He deserved better, and if Wade had anything to say about it, he was going to make sure he got it.

"You want to be with me. You're *sure*."

"Tristan," Wade said firmly, "I've never been more sure of anything. Even playin' football, so that should tell you something."

"What if one of us doesn't make the team?" Tristan questioned.

"You can't talk that way, because that's not the way it's happening." Wade knew he could dig in about things, about things he really wanted, but this felt even more absolute.

They were going to make the team.

Both of them.

No matter what happened, they were going to have that.

"You're being stubborn," Tristan claimed, but he was smiling. Like he couldn't help himself, and Wade would have to be a lot stupider not to love that.

"Yeah, but that's okay, because it's your kinda stubborn," Wade retorted.

"What if *neither* of us make the team because we do this?"

"Is that really what you think is going to happen?" Wade pulled on a t-shirt.

Tristan worried his bottom lip. Wade wanted to lean in and bite it for him, but he didn't. This was a big decision. He already knew what Tristan was going through though, because he'd been just as helpless to resist. And once he'd fallen, he was going to do everything in his power to make sure they both got what they deserved.

Each other.

And two spots on the final Piranhas roster.

"No . . ." Tristan admitted. "No."

Wade put his hands on his guy's shoulders. Squeezed. "And if it does, then it does. But I feel like I've been standing around, my whole life, just waiting, and now I'm not waiting anymore."

"Because of me?"

"Because of you." Everyone always talked about how expressing your feelings was tough, but Wade was beginning to figure out that they were full of shit. He hadn't been able to do it before, because he hadn't felt anything worth expressing before. But now, when he did?

He wanted to tell Tristan everything.

"Huh," Tristan said slowly. "So this is what this feels like."

"What *what* feels like?"

Tristan reached up and pressed a quick kiss to his mouth. "A relationship," he said, "with someone I can depend on."

"Thick and thin, sweetcheeks," Wade reassured him.

Tristan smiled. "I hate that nickname."

"Oh, I know," Wade retorted. "But you kinda love it, too."

And maybe it was crazy, but it was their kind of crazy and right now, in this cheap college dorm room, that was all that mattered.

They were in this together, and as far as Wade was concerned, they were both making the team.

Wade's confidence, always a beautiful thing, was stunning to behold at that afternoon's practice.

Some of it was inevitably Beau's tips that he'd passed on during their last few film sessions, because Tristan recognized some of the moves he was making.

He didn't quite have the spin move down, not the way that Tristan did, because Tristan was quicker, had less bulk to shift

around, but he was still evading Sebastian like his life depend-
ed on it.

And, Tristan thought as he watched him, maybe it did.

At least the life that he thought they might both want.

"That move you pulled earlier on Sea Bass was a thing of
beauty," Beau said, and Tristan looked over as the guy walked
up next to him. The last time they'd spoken had been early
this morning, when he'd walked in, uninvited, to see him and
Wade in each other's arms.

Beau had been present at the informal practice he'd come
to tell them about, of course, but he hadn't directly spoken to
either of them, other than a few shouted instructions.

But now, he was here, and despite all the confidence oozing
out of Wade, Tristan found he was still apprehensive.

"Thanks," Tristan said. "I . . . uh . . . about this morning."

Beau waved his hand. "Don't worry about it."

"I appreciate you waiting until . . . well, until it's the right
time."

"Is there ever a right time to fall for the wrong person?"
Beau's smile was wry.

Tristan laughed, in spite of the anxiety spiking in his stomach. "No."

"Honestly, it's not my business. It's not *our* business. Our business is to put the best possible team together and to win football games." Beau hesitated. "I like to think you guys know what
you're doing and us being restrictive assholes only makes things

tougher. I don't care if you're happy, as long as you're still hungry to win."

"We're both goddamn starving," Tristan said.

Beau cracked a smile and slapped him on the back. Tilted his head towards the field, where Coach Randy was beckoning the second group of receivers in for drills. "Then get your hungry ass out there and show Howard what the new generation plays like."

Tristan nodded, and jogged out, passing Wade on the way.

Their eyes met, blue greeting gray, and it was both silly and impossible for Tristan to feel *better* just by seeing him, by seeing his confidence, but he did, anyway.

Coach Randy went over the drill, and Tristan adjusted his gloves.

He'd yet to drop a pass in one of these, even the long ones, and he knew there were a ton of eyes on him as he set his feet, readying to sprint downfield.

It had been this way the whole camp so far.

At first, he knew they'd been watching and waiting for him to fail. To show how he couldn't evade an NFL-caliber defense because he hadn't played at the most elite level in college.

Now, he knew they were watching because he'd surpassed their expectations, and they were curious what he *could* do.

A whole goddamn lot, Tristan thought, and Coach Randy blew the whistle, and as he sprinted down the field, wind whistling in his ears, his eyes tracked Pax's movements, watched him pull back his arm and let the ball fly hard and deep.

He adjusted and then adjusted again, the wind changing the ball's trajectory. It was a tough throw—across Pax's left side, requiring an unbelievable amount of arm strength and pinpoint accuracy, but as the ball touched Tristan's hands, he believed, not for the first time, that they were going to make a dynamite pair in the NFL.

There was a round of applause echoing around the field as he jogged back to the starting line.

"That was a fucking dynamite route," Coach Randy said, patting him on the back. "More like that, please."

"I've got all you want," Tristan said with a grin.

"Seriously, great catch," Pax said.

"Seriously," Tristan retorted, "great *throw*."

"Well, let's see some more," Coach Randy said, and this time gestured to where Sebastian was stretching on the sidelines. "With some coverage, this time."

This was what he'd been practicing for. Getting up early and staying at practice late. Watching film with Beau.

Beau had warned him that Sea Bass would adjust to his moves, and he was right, but this time, as they sprinted across the field, he waited a split second longer, thighs pumping and straining, and he stopped suddenly and curled around the other side. Beau unleashed the ball, and he caught it, barely evading Sebastian's grasp as he crossed the drill line.

Coach Randy was clapping again as they returned to the huddle.

"Good job, good job, he's gonna keep you on your toes," Coach said to Sebastian.

"Not just my goddamn toes," Sebastian muttered under his breath. "*Goddamn.*"

"Feeling it this morning?" Tristan teased.

"I'm feeling some kind of way," Sebastian claimed.

"Old, that's what you're feeling. It's *old*," Beau chimed in as he walked over.

Sebastian frowned. "*Old*? I'll show you fucking old."

Coach was talking to Pax and Abernathy, going over some adjustments to the next drill, and Wade sidled over as Tristan kept himself loose and limber. "I think Beau is trying to start some shit," Wade said under his breath. "Or maybe he's trying to push both of us. I don't fucking know."

"I'm not sure," Tristan said. "But we're looking good today."

Wade gave him an appraising look. "Yeah, you are."

Tristan elbowed him lightly in the side. "Save it for the room, dude, we're working here."

Wade laughed. "I thought you were running circles around Sebastian Howard. Is that work? Or is it play? I'm not sure."

Tristan couldn't help his grin. "Kinda feels like both."

"Don't worry, I'm sure Coach'll come up with some new kind of torture this afternoon."

They were only a few days away from the walk-through for the Hall of Fame game, the opening game of the new season, so it was inevitable that Coach would keep coming up with new wrinkles, new plays, new ways to test them.

Their performance at the Hall of Fame game wouldn't guarantee them a spot on the roster, but if they both played well, Tristan knew they'd have passed the first—and most important—test.

They could hang with other players in the NFL.

Everything else would just be gravy.

Of course, if Coach Dawson decided that they couldn't be together and play together, that would be another story, but Tristan pushed that thought away. That was an anxiety for another day.

Today, the sun was shining and he was playing great football *and* he had a boyfriend.

One who believed in him and *them* like he'd never experienced before.

They broke for lunch after a few more drills, but instead of going to the cafeteria, Wade, Tristan and a few other receivers, like Carter Johnson, went to Beau's office, where he had the Steelers film from their last few games pulled up.

The Steelers were the opposing team in the Hall of Fame game, and Beau had offered to give them some additional pointers.

For Tristan and Wade it had been a no-brainer. They weren't going to pass up any extra chances to get ahead, not now, not when this was already important, and had become even more in the last few days.

"So," Beau said, his mouth full of sandwich, using his pointer to select one of the Steelers' defensive backs, "you can see that they tend to press the quarterback, so Pax is going to be getting the ball out quick. Probably not a lot of chances for deep balls—sorry, Tristan—*but* the key with them is going to be extending the play. Their corners aren't as good as their backs. If you can get loose and fast, you're going to have a chance at first downs, and more."

"That's alright with me, 'cause if I can get free, I can outrun any of their corners," Tristan said. It wasn't really cocky, though maybe he'd caught some of Wade's confidence, but the truth.

There were very few corners in the National Football League that he couldn't flat-out outrun.

But Beau was going to be right, Tristan thought as Beau cycled through some additional film, Pax was going to be under fire all game. He was going to be throwing short outs, most likely a lot of them to Wade, or to the slot receivers.

Carter was a mixture of both a deep and a slot receiver, and he was basically a lock to make the team, as he'd been the Piranhas' number one receiver for the last few years. But Tristan knew that if he wanted to make that number-two spot his—or worst-case scenario, the number slot—he was going to need to get free and get some yards after the catch during this game. Make a strong first impression. He made a mental note to work on some of his routes post-catch at the next few practices.

He had the speed, now he just needed to add the smarts.

"Can you pull up some more corner coverage?" Tristan asked Beau between bites of his own macaroni and cheese. He'd made weight, the last few days, but he was not averse to bulking up a bit more.

The Steelers were aggressive because they played in an aggressive division. He didn't want to be easy to push around.

"Yeah, of course," Beau said, and clicked the screen. Tristan studied the play quietly, watching as it unfolded, DeAndre Hopkins from the Texans who was normally the kind of deep receiver that Tristan was, dodged a middle linebacker, and then cut through the zone, and then, did a little cut to avoid the corner covering him, and caught the ball mid-stride, taking it for another twenty-five yards.

"That," Beau said, gesturing, "is what you're gonna need to do. Be smarter than them. Tougher, too."

"Tougher than the Steelers?" Carter laughed. "Yeah, that'll be the day."

Tristan could see the frown forming on Wade's face almost before it happened. Prayed that he wouldn't say anything or intervene because the surest way for Tristan to deal with Carter's bullshit was to face it *himself,* head-on, without flinching.

"That wasn't what Sea Bass was complaining about earlier," Tristan said, meeting Carter's eyes with a firm, confident gaze. He wasn't going to be scared off. Because the likeliest cause of all this bullshit was that Carter himself was intimidated. By Tristan. And that had to mean he was doing a lot of things right.

"Yeah, yeah," Carter said, waving a hand.

It probably wasn't the last time Carter was going to give him shit, but Tristan had believed before that he could handle it and now he knew he could.

The frown lines smoothed off Wade's face and he shot Tristan a quiet smile that was proud and full of more of that unquenchable confidence.

Like he'd known, even though Carter had pissed him off plenty, that Tristan could deal with it.

The lunch meeting broke up after that, and they had a few hours before the afternoon practice, which Tristan already knew was going to be full of intensity and pressure.

The coaching staff knew their first game was coming up, and they wouldn't take it easy on them.

After dropping their plates off in the cafeteria, Wade leaned in, and said under his breath, "You wanna go back for a nice cuddle in the room before the afternoon's insanity?"

Tristan nodded.

They'd returned their mattresses to their separate bedstands after Beau had found them this morning, but it was easy enough to drag them back together, and they resumed nearly the same position they'd been in this morning.

Tristan wasn't quite ready to sleep yet, and he was scrolling through Instagram. It occurred to him that he hadn't posted in almost two weeks.

Before camp, and before Wade, his first instinct had always been to post. He'd grown a huge audience—and he'd argue he'd become influential with a group who didn't just want the representation but *needed* it—but it felt good to not have to live his life on social media.

Alec had told him that he'd eventually get there; using it and not letting it use *him*, but he hadn't expected that it would happen so quickly or painlessly.

Or that he wouldn't miss it at all.

"Wade?" Tristan asked uncertainly, not sure if he was still awake.

"Yeah?" Wade's voice was sleepy.

Tristan turned his head and shifted so he could look into Wade's eyes. "You know what you said this morning, about feeling like you were just standing around, waiting for your life to begin?"

Wade nodded.

"I think . . . me too."

There was no denying it; Wade looked floored by Tristan's admission.

"But you're Tristan Nicholson. You're influential. You've got all those followers. You're a beacon of hope for so many people."

"It turns out it's pretty easy to start out as a beacon of hope and have that turn into something else. Your whole identity, actually. I didn't know who I was apart from Tristan Nicholson, influencer."

"And now?" There was no judgment in Wade's voice.

It was one of the things that Tristan liked so goddamn much about him.

One of *many* things.

"Now . . . I think I'm finding my way."

"Camp's been hard so far, but I think the good kind of hard," Wade said, and there was a deep satisfaction in his tone, one that echoed through Tristan.

He felt it too.

This had been one of the hardest things he'd ever done.

He'd always been really good at football. Good at catching passes. Really good at being the fastest guy on the team.

He'd never had to struggle or work all that hard. He'd always just been the best, natural as breathing.

It was inevitable that when he was drafted, that would change. Alec had told him the blunt truth when he'd signed with him—that it would be an uphill climb to be taken seriously and it was likely he wouldn't be drafted high—but it had been a rude awakening to be drafted in the fifth round. He'd never expected to fall that low.

He'd known then that he had work to do.

Then this summer, working out with Alec's guys, the same thing. When Pax had told him he had to run a better route, at first he'd been pissed, and then he'd gotten stubborn.

He was going to learn. He could learn how to do anything.

And he had.

Now Coach Randy wasn't yelling at him every other drill about taking the shittiest route, he was encouraging, and Tristan had actually managed to evade *the* Sebastian Howard on more than one occasion.

Tristan digested all of this and said after a long silence, "I guess if we really wanted to make it hard, we could've not kissed that first time."

Wade chuckled and his arm tightened around Tristan, fingers drifting lower on his back. "That's cute, sweetcheeks. But it wasn't ever gonna happen. I saw you, and I wanted you. Like I hadn't ever wanted anyone else before. Ain't no hard or easy or in-between about it. Some things are just meant to be."

"What if Beau hadn't made us roommates?"

"I think . . ." Wade hesitated. "I think Beau Dawson is real smart and he does things for a reason. I think he knew what would be good for us. And it was each other. From the start."

"Hmmm," Tristan considered, and lay back down on Wade's chest.

He had a feeling that his life was going to change very drastically in the next few weeks, and he might not recognize it at all when all the upheaval ended. But the one thing he was certain of was that he was going to face it with the one person he trusted completely.

Chapter Eight

It was the last full-impact practice before the Piranhas—all ninety-two of them, plus support and coaching staff—got on the plane and headed towards Canton, Ohio, and the Football Hall of Fame, which hosted the annual Hall of Fame at the beginning of each season.

Wade didn't think it would be the most important game of his career. After all, he had hopes of winning a Super Bowl someday. There'd be games with rivals, and hopefully playoff games, and maybe even *the* game, which decided the best team in the NFL. But before any of that, he had to play and succeed in *this* game.

He told himself that was why he was a little on edge this afternoon.

Not because he'd been stuck blocking for most of the practice.

He was great at blocking, but he could do so much more.

When he'd said something two plays ago to Coach Randy, he'd not been dismissive exactly, because there was a look of quiet confidence in his gaze when he looked at Wade—like he knew what Wade was capable of and that was plenty to win his approval.

So, he'd probably make the team, unless he monumentally fucked up.

That didn't mean he didn't want to do *more*.

Tristan, on the other hand, was getting yet another workout.

He was lined up nearly every play opposite Sebastian, and he was killing it, running great routes, and not evading the great Sea Bass every play, but enough that it was obvious how far he'd come since camp had begun.

Wade couldn't help but be proud, and *also* wish that he could get some of that for himself.

"Huddle up," Pax called out, and the offense formed a loose circle around their quarterback. They were running special package plays, perfecting them before the game in two days—like fourth-down plays, and two-point conversions—and there was always a unique wrinkle that made them difficult to execute well.

"Here's the play," Pax said, and read it off his wristband. "You got it?"

Wade took in the nods around the group, and met Tristan's eyes. He was breathing hard, a sheen of sweat on his forearms, and Wade was glad to see that he wouldn't be running the length of the field *again*. This play called for a five-receiver set—including Wade, *finally*—and was supposed to be an alternative to a run play on fourth down.

He lined up, making a quick note where Sea Bass was, and when Coach Randy blew the whistle, he let his mind go blissfully blank as he sprinted off the line, the ball snapping to his left, Pax catching it and dropping back confidently.

The idea was that all five receivers would run routes close to the first-down marker, making it tough for the defense to cover everyone adequately, and Pax would pick the uncovered guy, converting the fourth down to a first down.

Wade realized almost immediately that one of the better defensive backs was elevated in the zone, covering him. He might be a big guy, but Markus Andrews was bigger, and *fast*, and unfortunately gaining on him, covering him pretty well, considering he was a defensive end and pass coverage wasn't going to ever be his strong suit.

Wade changed positions twice, curling to the right, and then dodging to the left, hanging right around the first-down marker, hoping that Pax might decide to throw him the ball anyway, but it was immediately obvious that he wasn't going to.

He had Tristan in his sights, who was being covered by a linebacker, which was exactly the matchup that Wade would've expected him to exploit. Tyler Jenkins, the linebacker covering Tristan was strong, but he was slow, and Tristan evaded him easily, weaving a route right around him.

Pax let the ball fly and Tristan snagged it right out of the air, easily getting the first down, and Wade saw out of the corner of his eye, also an approving nod from Coach Randy.

Tyler Jenkins was an older player, maybe in his thirties if Wade remembered correctly, and though he'd had a decent career earlier on, was probably in danger of not making the team.

Tristan had already caught the ball for a first down, so even though tackling was *technically* permitted in contested plays during the second, padded practice of the day, it was mostly discouraged.

Nobody wanted their players to get hurt in *practice*.

But Tyler Jenkins clearly didn't give a shit about that, because instead of letting the play go dead, as anyone else would have, he tackled Tristan to the ground with a hard, bruising grip, pushing him relentlessly into the turf.

Wade, a few yards away, heard Tristan's surprised *ooomph*, and he couldn't help but hear the muttered homophobic nastiness spewing out of Jenkins' mouth right after he tackled him mercilessly to the turf.

It was just a few words but it was enough.

Wade's jaw dropped open.

He'd always heard rumors that life in the NFL for queer players was still not a walk in the park, despite all the progress that players like Colin O'Connor and Spencer Evans and Heath Harris and Sam Crawford had made.

But he'd not gotten a whiff of it, not at the combine, not at rookie mini camp this summer, and definitely not at preseason camp. Not until now.

Jenkins took some time getting up, and didn't offer a hand to Tristan.

Wade almost jogged over and offered his guy a hand, but he was afraid if he did, he would punch Jenkins in the face.

And that would definitely mean he wouldn't make the Piranhas' final roster.

Punching your teammates, even when they happened to be homophobic dirtbags, was unsurprisingly frowned upon.

Tristan stood, and stretched. His face was grim, and that same expression was on every person's face around them.

Pax looked shocked. Sea Bass looked furious.

And then, Beau jogged over.

"What the fuck was that?" he demanded to know of Jenkins.

Jenkins just shrugged, like he didn't believe he had to answer to the head coach's queer son.

That was the moment things got *really* ugly.

Coach Dawson walked—no, Wade corrected, he *stalked*—onto the field and right up to where Jenkins stood, seemingly unconcerned that he'd just wildly insulted not only a possible player on the team but the coach's own son.

Coach didn't say a word until he was nearly on top of Jenkins.

Then he shoved his hands into his pockets and regarded him like a wolf might regard a particularly vulnerable, particularly tasty snack.

Wade knew he wasn't the only one on the field holding his breath.

"Care to repeat what you just said," Coach said in a low, slow drawl. "Not sure the whole team heard you."

Smartly, Jenkins went white around the edges.

"Uh," he stammered.

"What was that?" Coach said, his tone suddenly sharp and demanding. "I didn't quite hear that either."

Jenkins mumbled something that Wade couldn't quite make out.

"I'd make you run sprints just for that shitty, stupid tackle your ego demanded you make," Coach said. "But then you added insult to injury and said something I *do not permit* on this team."

His tanned face looked like it had been carved from marble. It was inexorable. And Wade was suddenly reminded that Asa Dawson was the iron fist of this team. The iron fist of a leader who had won fifteen SEC Championships, and five National Championships. A legend, who did not take crap from anyone.

Especially a bug on his shoe, like Jenkins.

"I didn't . . ." Jenkins was still stumbling over his words.

"You did," Coach said. "You absolutely fucking did, and so you can go clean out your locker. Security is going to make sure you're off campus within the hour. I don't ever want to see your face again."

"But . . ."

But Coach Dawson was already turning around, leaving Jenkins behind. Mentally. Physically. In every single way you could leave a person.

Jenkins' shoulders slumped, but Wade didn't feel an ounce of sympathy, and he didn't see many faces that looked particularly disappointed either.

Sebastian had a surprised, contemplative look on his face, and Wade wondered again if Tristan had been right, and he was queer, too.

"I do not permit that kind of language on this team," Coach said, meeting the rest of his players' eyes while raising his voice effortlessly. It carried to every inch of the field and the sidelines, too.

"I don't permit homophobic bullshit. I don't permit bullying. I permit you to play good fucking football and nothing else. If you wanna start some shit, go someplace else. I don't got the patience for it. What Jenkins here," Coach continued, referring to Tyler Jenkins like he wasn't still there, looking floored, like he'd never imagined that the most successful coach in SEC history would ever turn out to be so progressive, "doesn't understand is that change is coming. Fuck, change is already here. You either learn to adjust to that change, to believe that the guy next to you can play just as well as you, no matter who he loves, or you can leave."

Coach pinned each and every one of them around him with a look that brokered absolutely no argument. "And," he added, "we won't miss you."

He turned and left, leaving Jenkins still gaping.

"Beau," he added, without even a glance backwards, "make sure to call security, there's some trash that needs cleaned up on this field."

Beau pulled his phone out of his pocket, made a quick call, and then after consulting briefly with Coach Randy, jogged off after his dad.

Coach Randy clapped, and suddenly, they were back at practice, like the confrontation had never happened.

Tristan approached, shaking off the hit still.

"You okay, Nicholson?" Coach Randy asked, his voice softening a bit. "If you need to take the next play off . . ."

But Tristan gave himself a final shake and shook his head firmly. "I'm fine. I can come in, no problem."

"Okay," Coach said.

They finished the practice. Another defensive end took Jenkins' place, and that was that.

But even though Tristan seemed to have shaken off the incident, Wade couldn't.

Even after he got out of the shower, and changed into sweatpants and a t-shirt, perfect for lounging around until dinner, he couldn't stop his brain from thinking about it.

That could've been him.

While he'd been at camp, and while he'd been with Tristan, he'd thought more than once that if he was being honest with himself, he might as well be honest with others, too. And if he'd gone with his instincts, *and* told people, that could've been him.

If Jenkins had felt secure enough doing that kind of shit in practice, in front of God and everybody, what would he have felt comfortable doing if he'd managed to confront Tristan alone?

Wade felt a wave of nausea crest through him, making him feel shaky and uneasy.

Was this how it felt to come out? To never know who wanted to secretly—or not so secretly—kick your ass?

"Hey," Tristan said, coming up next to him. "You gonna get some dinner?" He put a hand on Wade's back—a gesture that many of the more touchy-feely players wouldn't have blinked at twice—but now he felt weird about.

They weren't *hiding*, not really, though Wade knew the first person they were going to need to tell was Coach Dawson. But the fact that Tristan touching him made him apprehensive made him want to find the nearest trash can and vomit.

Then there was the fact Jenkins could've really hurt Tristan.

That made him even sicker, *and* it made him fucking mad as hell.

"How can you think about eating right now?"

Wade heard the ache of anxiety in his own voice, but Tristan was still smiling as he shrugged. "Well, we had a long-ass weightlifting session this morning and two practices, where I probably sprinted the length of the field a dozen times at least, so *yeah*, I could definitely eat."

"I mean . . . aren't you *bothered*?"

Tristan curled his fingers into Wade's bicep. "You wanna talk about it?"

"Don't you?"

Tristan shrugged again. "Shit happens, okay? It's not the first time someone's called me that, and it won't be the last. If I let it bother me every time, I'd never get up in the morning, never put my uniform on, never jog out onto the field, under the lights I love so much. I won't let those assholes win and keep me from doing any of those things, so I learned to ignore them."

"How?" Wade knew how plaintive he sounded. "I want to throw up. I want to pound his face in. I want to . . ." He hesitated. "I want to cry."

"That . . . that doesn't always get better, but it does, at the same time. Does that make sense? You get better at managing the emotion of it."

"Do you really?"

"Yes," Tristan said with certainty. "Yes, it *will* get easier. And you know what? You don't *have* to tell anybody. You don't owe anyone a goddamn thing."

"But then we're hiding. You're hiding." It was the thing that had worried Wade, back in the corners of his mind, from the beginning. He didn't want to shove Tristan back into the closet. He didn't want to force him to hide. But was he ready to expose his truth to everyone's judgement? He didn't know.

"Yeah, but it's not forever," Tristan said, rolling his eyes. "I think there's plenty of benefits for me, no matter what the cost."

Wade wanted to believe him.

But he knew enough about the pressures of living a lie, and how easy it was for those pressures to destroy relationships.

He didn't want to lose Tristan before they'd barely begun.

"But if I wanted . . ." Wade swallowed hard. He could barely get the words out from his uncooperative mouth.

"Hey, I mean it," Tristan said softly, and reached out again, gripping his arm. It wasn't quite as good as holding hands, but it was as close as they could do in the locker room. "You're still figuring your shit out. What kind of boyfriend would I be if I didn't have any patience?"

"What about your social media?" Wade knew it was a mistake the moment he'd asked the question. The open honesty on Tristan's face shuttered, almost immediately.

"What about it?"

"I mean . . . isn't that part of your brand?" Wade wanted to smack himself in the face. He wasn't doing himself any favors. He knew it. And even if he hadn't known it, the way Tristan looked would have told him everything. "Don't you need to be honest or something? About your relationships? About me?"

"I don't need to do anything." Tristan took a deep, shuddering breath. "Listen, I *know* you're not telling me that all I am is my Instagram feed, but . . . well, I don't like being reduced to that. That, it's not me. *This* is me."

"I know that." Wade hoped that Tristan believed him.

Tristan's expression softened. "I know you do. I get what you're saying. How does it look later when people find out that I've been dating a closeted player? Especially when I've been so outspoken? You know what it looks like? That I fell for someone who wasn't ready. Not everyone has to be ready right away, Wade. That's not a requirement. When I post, I'm not trying to tell everyone that they have to be ready *now*, I'm telling them that they'll have my unconditional support when they are ready."

Wade felt his lungs begin to loosen a little. "Okay."

"Seriously, you're fine. We're fine." Tristan smiled again and elbowed him teasingly in the ribs. "Now come on, let's grab some dinner before I do something unforgivably unmanly and pass out from hunger and exhaustion."

"I think . . ." Wade paused, and to his own surprise, the nausea had passed. There was still the echo of the anger, pressed deep inside of him, but the sickly feeling that had haunted him since he'd heard Jenkins taunt Tristan had passed. "I think I could go for some dinner."

Tristan's grin was so bright, it was blinding. "Told you," he said. "Someday you're gonna figure out that I'm always right."

"Someday?" Wade teased right back. For a single blinding second, he wished that Tristan would slide his hand down, until it met his own, and they would walk hand in hand to the dining hall, damn anyone who would say a word.

He didn't, because he knew he wasn't quite ready yet—and they hadn't told Coach Dawson yet. Wade wasn't stupid enough to think he shouldn't be the first to find out.

But he knew he'd be ready someday.

Maybe even someday soon.

Chapter Nine

Alec called him the night before they flew out of Canton. "I've been hearing good things about you from camp," he said.

"You have?" Tristan wasn't really surprised; he had gotten a *lot* better in the last few weeks.

Wade had been a big part of that, but also Beau, and Coach Randy, and having a great quarterback like Pax, which always made him want to *be* better.

It was a dynamite combination, pushing him and challenging him, and Tristan could look back on his last few years playing college ball and realize that he *hadn't* been good enough. He'd been resting on his natural skill.

He wasn't doing that anymore.

"You've worked hard," Alec said, "but then, I knew you would."

"If I didn't, I might as well just have given up and never showed up at camp in the first place," Tristan said.

"And," Alec added then, "I haven't seen you post anything on your Instagram in awhile, either."

"Too busy with camp." What he should do was tell Alec about Wade, but he found himself hesitating.

Alec would understand—probably. After all, he was dating the great Spencer Evans, who also happened to be a client of his.

He'd understand that sometimes the heart wouldn't be contained, that it wouldn't listen to what was prudent, that it liked to go off the rails and pick the least appropriate person to fall for.

"Well, no matter what the reason, I think it's a good call," Alec said.

"Thanks," Tristan said wryly. "It wasn't so much a call as . . . well, a necessity. There's not a lot of time here to develop social media content."

"That could be, but no matter what, you've made the right choice, focusing on your career. If you wanted to be a professional influencer, you could've done that. But you wanted to play football. So you're playing football, and apparently really damn well, too."

One of the reasons why Tristan had chosen Alec to represent him had been his lack of sugarcoating. The fact that he was one of the few out and proud gay agents in the sport was another. But mostly, Tristan just respected the hell out of how good he was at his job.

"Let me know if you hear anything else," Tristan said.

"You mean, anything other than apparently you're Beau Dawson's new pet project?" Alec chuckled. "I will."

He'd just gotten off the phone when Wade had come back into the room, apparently having had a conversation of his own.

"I told my dad about me," Wade said, sitting down heavily on the edge of the mattress. "He was . . . not surprised, and not mad, actually. Just . . . I thought it would be worse."

"It's not always worse," Tristan said, wrapping an arm around him. "And you didn't know how he'd react. He's in the military, right?"

"He's an Air Force general. He said, as long as I work hard, it shouldn't matter who I love." Wade's eyes grew softer then, and Tristan wondered, his breath catching, if Wade could *love* him. It was so early, but he was feeling things he hadn't ever experienced yet, so maybe it was possible.

"I'm glad it wasn't terrible," Tristan said. "And congrats on coming out again."

"Is it this hard every time?"

"Do you mean, will telling Coach Dawson be as hard as telling your dad? Probably not. Though he might yell more."

Wade grinned. "Because he's gonna find out that we're together. That's why he's gonna yell."

Tristan shrugged, though that did seem very likely.

"I did tell him—my dad," Wade clarified, "about us. Or that I'd met someone here at camp, and I really, really liked them. That was what shocked me the most. That he said he wasn't surprised. I guess there were always people in his divisions that fell for each other, because they were spending so much time together it was inevitable."

"Huh," Tristan said. He hadn't thought of it that way, probably because he hadn't fallen for Wade because of their close proximity. That had certainly moved things along faster, but he'd fallen for Wade because he was . . . well, because he was Wade.

He was handsome and kind and loyal and confident and shone with goodness. And he had a wicked tongue—both when he told a joke, and when he used it to make Tristan moan. It was all those things and more that had made Wade Lewis irresistible.

"Anyway, I think . . . I think it went well." Wade sounded surprised, but pleased. Relieved, more like, and that tension he'd sensed in him since the Tyler Jenkins incident seemed to ease out of him a little bit more.

By the time they left for the Hall of Fame game, traveling from a private airstrip outside the Orlando airport to Canton, Ohio, Tristan was relieved that Wade seemed to settle.

It wasn't like he hadn't cared that Tyler Jenkins had turned out to be an asshole, or that those words hadn't hurt him. They always hurt. But what he'd told Wade had been true; he wasn't going to let jerks like Jenkins stop him from accomplishing everything he wanted.

He'd worried that Wade wouldn't be able to shake it off, and Jenkins' homophobic shit would stop him from playing well in the game.

But by the time they boarded the plane, his smiles were coming readily again, and when Tristan told a joke, he laughed without hesitation.

When they warmed up together, wearing their Piranhas jerseys for the first time, there was the fire that Tristan recognized blazing in Wade's eyes.

He wanted this.

Just as badly as Tristan did.

And Tristan knew they were going to get it done.

During the walk-through yesterday, Coach Randy had made it clear that they would both be getting significant playing time.

Unsaid had been the assumption that if they played well, the path to making the team became a hell of a lot easier.

The Steelers were a very good football team, and it would have been stupid to underestimate them. The first offensive drive, Tristan felt a rush of sudden, inexplicable nerves as he jogged out onto the field, Wade next to him.

In the huddle, Pax's eyes were serious.

There was a lot riding on this game—and on this season.

Tristan understood what it was like to have everyone believe the worst of you, and also the overriding need to prove them all wrong.

Coach Dawson felt it.

Beau felt it.

Pax felt it.

God knew, Davis Abernathy and his ring-less fingers felt it.

But Tristan—and Wade—did too.

That burning need in the base of his stomach calmed the nerves, and by the time the huddle broke up, the Piranhas ready to run the first offensive play of the new season, he was ready.

He'd never been more ready in his whole goddamned life.

So ready that when the ball snapped, and he ran his first route, it felt like his feet were flying across the field. The Steelers' corner on this side was not nearly as good as Sea Bass was, and Tristan lost him with a little curl to the left, then moving to the right, twelve yards from the line of scrimmage. Pax unloaded the ball with a quick slant, and Tristan's fingers closed around it, giving himself that extra split second to make sure he had it, before he turned on his heel, digging into the turf, and began to run.

The Steelers' new safety was not as good as Troy Polamalu had been—but then what safety was?—but he took a good angle, and after Tristan passed the fifteen-yard mark, a solid first down effort, he braced himself for the impact.

At the last moment, he spun away, losing a little of his speed, but evading the tackle of the safety meant that he could turn up field and there was not a single player between him and the end zone.

Of course, he was fast, but there were fast players on the Steelers' defense too, and he could feel them churning behind him as he sprinted the last twenty yards, but he did it anyway, his lungs burning and his muscles cramping.

Tristan crossed the line, his fingers digging into the football, not stupid enough to let it go, because this was his first NFL touchdown.

He'd scored a touchdown. In the NFL. On his very first freaking play.

There was an incredulous part of him, one that had understood why all those people had talked about him, like he couldn't really play football at an elite level, but then . . . there was the rest of him.

He'd known he could do it.

He'd just needed the opportunity.

The rest of the offense caught up to him in the end zone.

Wade was first, pulling him into a hug, his smile bright even through the face mask of his helmet. Pride shining undeniably in his eyes.

"Fuck yeah," he crowed as he pulled Tristan in. "You fucking did it."

Pax and the offensive line were next, a jumbled celebration of joy.

Everyone felt it.

Defenses were going to pay attention now.

But they'd gotten over the first hump.

The rest of the game passed in a blur.

Wade scored a highly contested touchdown in the third quarter, battling through three defensive players to just get the ball past the line.

Just as Tristan's touchdown had been a fantastic example of his explosive potential every time he stepped onto the field, Wade's had highlighted exactly what he was good at: being tough and big and impossible to bring down. He never gave up on the play, even when the odds were nearly insurmountable, and Tristan made sure he was first to the end zone to congratulate him.

By the time the last few seconds of the fourth quarter were ticking away, the Piranhas had scored forty-one points, Tristan had almost two hundred yards receiving and the touchdown, and Wade had the touchdown of his own, as well as several first downs under his belt, and almost a hundred yards receiving of his own.

For a tight end, it was a brilliant performance.

They were sitting on the sideline bench, watching as the Steelers pointlessly ran one last drive, when Beau came up to them, giving them each a high five.

"I knew you two could pull it off," he said, crouching low in front of them. "That was fucking badass."

Tristan grinned. It wasn't an absolute guarantee they'd both make the team, but it was as close to a guarantee as one got in the NFL. They'd been given an opportunity and they'd both made the most of it.

It had taken them a hell of a lot of work to get there, and Tristan still couldn't quite believe that they'd pulled it off.

But he already knew that the footage of his touchdown was going to be on all the sports shows, playing over and over again on ESPN.

He'd make the team.

Not just because he was a damn good football player, but because he was good for business. Tristan knew that, and decided, even, that he didn't much care, as long as he got to keep playing, and got to keep doing it with Wade at his side.

"And," Beau added, "don't think I didn't see that key block you made, Lewis, keeping that defensive end from tackling Tristan before he could get loose on that first touchdown play."

Tristan looked over at his boyfriend. "You did what?"

But Wade only shrugged modestly. "Anyone else would've blocked that guy too."

"Not as well as you did," Beau said. "Let's watch the film tonight, when we get back."

Tristan and Wade exchanged glances. "Yeah, I think we're going to be a little busy," Tristan said, and Beau laughed.

"I bet you are," Beau said, "but still, I wanna see you guys for a minute. And I know my dad will too."

"Coach?" Wade sounded apprehensive.

"It's not a done deal yet, but well, I can hardly imagine that any coach with sense would cut you after today. As long as you keep playing well and contributing, you've got a spot here. Welcome to the Piranhas." Beau extended a hand, and they both shook it, Wade first, and then Tristan.

"I think," Wade said under his breath as time expired and they stood, ready to head to the locker room, "that Beau wants us to tell his dad."

"Tonight?" Tristan had every intention of coming clean about their relationship to Coach Dawson, because anything less would be career suicide, but he also didn't intend to do it now.

Let the magnitude of their performances tonight sink in a bit further, before they tried to destroy all that hard work by revealing they'd done the one thing they weren't supposed to do: fall in love with each other.

Because Tristan knew now, at least for him, that was what it was. Without a doubt.

The moment he'd seen Wade's face in the end zone, he'd known it was the only one he ever wanted to see, and the truth had flashed through his heart like a goddamned spotlight, illuminating everything.

Maybe it was fast, but his feelings were real, and they weren't going away.

He was in love with Wade Lewis.

"I think we should," Wade said. "Beau is a smart guy. Smartest guy I know, anyway. If he thinks we should tell Coach now, then we should tell Coach now." He flopped down onto the bench in front of his locker. "I've never wanted to keep it a secret, anyway."

"I haven't either, but . . ."

"Listen," Wade said, and his eyes were intense, "it doesn't matter what he says. Nothing is going to change. They could drop me and I could sign in Los Angeles and I would still want to be with you, Tristan."

"That's not going to happen," Tristan argued, and then he knew that just like Beau, Wade was brilliant and had trapped him neatly in his own logic.

"Okay, fine," Tristan continued with a heavy sigh, tugging off his jersey, tossing it into the big laundry bin in the middle of the locker room. "We'll do it tonight. When we get back."

"And then after"—Wade's voice dropped even lower—"there's something I want to try. When we're alone."

Tristan's heart began to beat a little faster.

"What if . . . what if it doesn't go well, telling Coach?"

Wade just shrugged. "I'm still going to want you. I could be half-dead—I *have* been half-dead, actually—and I've always wanted you."

It was enough for Tristan.

"Alright," he said, casually, trying to pretend like he wasn't insatiably curious at what Wade wanted to try.

What he wanted to *do*.

The flight back to Orlando wasn't long, though the bus trip back to the South Orange campus was longer than Wade wanted.

He was antsy—not just because he'd agreed to tell Coach about his relationship with Tristan, but because of what else he was planning.

He couldn't wait to be alone with Tristan.

They'd shared plenty of hot nights together in the last two weeks, but Wade hadn't missed how Tristan was always being so careful of him and his sensibilities.

And while Wade appreciated how sensitive Tristan was to how new this all was—he wanted to give him something special.

Something he'd never done before.

He'd done a little research, and he knew what *he* liked, so hopefully he could make Tristan feel as good as Tristan always made him feel.

But now, there was one more task they had to complete before they could be alone, and Wade knew it wasn't going to be easy.

That wasn't the kind of coach that Coach Dawson was.

He expected great things. He expected total accountability. He expected complete commitment.

The very last thing Wade wanted to do was let him down.

Standing outside of Coach's partly open office door, Wade and Tristan exchanged a single look. Tristan looked a little terrified. Wade had a feeling that he was wearing a similar look. But instead of letting that fear control him, he controlled it. Reaching down, he took Tristan's hand and gripped it, hard.

"Come on," he said quietly.

With his free hand, Tristan knocked on the door.

"Come on in," Coach called out, and they pushed open the door together, walking in still holding hands.

Coach was on his laptop, glasses perched on the end of his nose, reading something intently. He didn't look up when they came in.

"What is it?" he asked, his tone not unfriendly but brusque. Because he was a head coach and God knew they were busy just about twenty-four hours a day.

"We wanted to talk to you," Wade said, "before you heard about it from someone else."

He glanced up then, his curiosity clearly piqued. "Heard about what?" he asked, and then Wade knew the moment he realized what it was and that the question would be irrelevant.

He sucked in a long, deep breath, and leaned back in his chair.

"So that's what it's like, huh?" Coach said thoughtfully. He didn't sound angry. Not yet.

"This is what it's like," Tristan said firmly. Confidently.

Wade, who felt like he was tipping right on the edge of falling head over heels, crazy in love, for this man, felt himself begin to slide over the cliff.

He knew how afraid Tristan was this would destroy everything, but when push came to shove, when it really mattered, he stood here, holding Wade's hand, head held high, met Coach's stare and he didn't flinch once.

Coach sighed. "Beau warned me that this was going to happen."

"He did?" Wade couldn't help but sound surprised.

"It's an emotional time." Coach waved. "There's a lot of heightened adrenaline responses going around because we're pushing you so hard. Also, he might have said something else, but I wasn't exactly listening."

"You weren't listening," Tristan stated, didn't ask. If Wade had sounded surprised, he sounded shocked.

"Nope." Coach grinned. "'Cause I don't give a shit. This distract you enough to stop you from doing anything you did tonight?"

"No, sir," Wade said.

"It gonna stop you in the future?" Coach asked bluntly.

"No, I can't imagine that it would," Tristan said.

"Then, I appreciate the honesty but I don't give a shit. Your private time is your private time."

"What if . . ." Wade hesitated. He still wasn't completely sure. He knew he might be ready soon, but it was impossible to say when he would be ready to stand in front of not only his coach, but the world, and hold Tristan's hand. "What if it wasn't just private?"

Coach's gaze turned speculative. "Want to tell everyone, huh?"

"Not like that," Tristan said hurriedly, and Wade realized a second later that he was worried that Coach was talking about his social media. "Not for attention. Just to be honest. We just want to be honest, eventually. If that's alright with you and with the team."

Coach waved a hand. "Just clear it with the PR people. I know it isn't the big deal it used to be, but they're gonna want a heads-up."

"Do . . . do you?"

Coach Dawson leaned forward, his elbows on the desk. It amazed Wade that anyone thought this man was stupid, hick accent or not. His eyes shone with intelligence. And then there was his son. "Not particularly, but if you want to give me one, that'd be nice."

"Nice." Tristan let out a big sigh, like the anxiety was rushing out of his body. "Nice. Huh, that is not what I expected you'd say."

"I'm not like those other coaches," Coach Dawson said. "I know people been talking about it, but it's true. It's not just a charade. I kinda have this radical idea that happy players are better players. Happiness makes you hungrier." He paused, and Wade felt like those eyes were taking him apart, molecule by molecule, like they truly wanted to understand him. "You feel any less hungry?"

"Nope, not even the slightest. In fact," Tristan said, glancing over at Wade, "I feel like we make each other better. We push each other to be better."

Coach nodded sharply. "That's what I want to hear. Now, go get some rest. It's been a long day, and you two have earned it." He paused, a sudden, unexpected smile emerging on his tanned face. "Earned a bunch more too. Expect to be on the field in September, if you keep playing like you did today."

"We will, you can count on it," Wade said fervently. It was more than he'd dared to hope for, and he was getting it, *and* the man he loved.

When he and Tristan walked out, he felt his heart soar.

"We did it," Tristan said quietly. Triumphantly.

"Yeah, we did," Wade said. Looked at the man next to him. The one who'd become so dear, so important. "Let's go celebrate, properly."

Wade would be lying to himself if he denied fantasizing about this for years. A guy, laid out in front of him, naked and aroused and wanting *him*.

Years ago, the guy had been faceless, just the general shape of muscles and skin with a kind smile. Just recently, in the last few weeks, the guy's features filled in. Sharp cheekbones, cinnamon-brown hair, the bluest eyes he'd ever seen, and a smile that was *still* kind but also undeniably mischievous. He was taller, taller than Wade had ever imagined, and he was a football player too. Maybe not as strong as Wade, but strong, still, the muscles in his arms and legs and chest rippling as Wade tugged down his underwear, removing the last piece of his clothing.

He'd also never imagined the way the guy would look at him—a mixture of caring and exasperation and arousal that made his tongue thick and his cock hard. But Tristan never failed to look at him that way, and Wade wanted to be on the receiving end of that look every morning and every night and every moment in between for as long as they could make this work.

Forever was a long time, and they'd just met, but once, Wade had asked his father how he'd known his mother was the "one."

"Just knew," he'd said ruefully. "Took one look at her, talked to her, and that was it. It could never be anyone else." What he'd said had resonated, because even after his mom had died, young, from breast cancer, his dad had never remarried.

And for Wade, there had never been anyone else, from his first glimpse of Tristan, to the first touch, to the first time they'd ever laughed together.

Wade couldn't imagine trusting anyone else this way, not to be at his most vulnerable.

"Now that I'm naked," Tristan teased, eyes twinkling, such a beautiful blue that Wade wanted to get lost in them forever, "what are your plans with me?"

"Just lie here, just like that," Wade said, sinking back on his heels. "I want to look at you for a moment." He hesitated. Sometimes he didn't know what all the rules were. Would Tristan be offended if he said what was in his heart? He didn't know. But the words didn't want to stay hidden. "You're beautiful, you know. Inside and out."

The teasing glint of Tristan's eyes softened. "Thank you."

"That's okay?"

"To tell me that I'm beautiful? And not just my face or my body, but my soul?" Tristan smiled, slow and sweet and true. "You can tell me that anytime you like."

"Then I will," Wade said. And he intended to, to tell Tristan how lucky he was every chance he could get.

"You're going to do more than just look, though, right?" Tristan suddenly looked apprehensive, and Wade realized he wasn't the only one who was a little bit nervous.

Somehow, Tristan's nerves helped alleviate Wade's.

He leaned forward and pressed his mouth to Tristan's lower stomach, feeling the soft skin there, laid over hard muscle. Reminding Wade of how sensitive Tristan could be, and also how strong. How he had a backbone made of steel and sheer, unrelenting will.

He spent a long minute nuzzling right where Tristan's hip met his stomach, where he was softest, and Tristan groaned as his tongue explored, loving the way he tasted.

"You're a tease," Tristan mumbled. "I didn't think you'd be a tease."

Wade raised his head. "You didn't think so?"

"Okay, maybe I would've, if I'd thought about it."

"This is all I've thought about, since you did it to me," Wade said reverently, ducking his head lower, his gaze level with Tristan's hard cock.

It was slightly curved, and bright red at the tip, twitching slightly as Wade stared at it.

"You don't have to . . ." Tristan's voice was breathless. "Not if you don't want to."

"Do you want me to?"

Tristan laughed wryly. "Is the sky blue?"

Wade didn't answer for himself, instead communicated his own desires by leaning in and licking up the side of Tristan's cock. Acclimating himself to the taste, to the weight of it on his tongue. He'd seen plenty of porn. Knew the basic actions. Had had this done to him enough times to understand how it worked.

But it was totally, unexpectedly, different to be on the giving end.

Not, Wade realized as he let the head slip into his mouth, hearing Tristan groan, in a bad way. In a really fucking good way, in fact.

He'd underestimated how much power you'd feel, when you were on your knees. How it felt to have a lover spread out in front of you, at your mercy.

To have *Tristan* spread out in front of him, trembling and trying to keep his noises quiet.

"I like this," Wade said, diving in again for another long suck, taking in a bit more this time, letting it slide into his mouth, curling his tongue around it.

"I like it too," Tristan retorted, panting. "Imagine that."

"I have been," Wade said quietly, and dove back in again.

For a long moment, there was nothing else but his mouth and his fingers, gripping Tristan's thighs, feeling the muscles tense in them as he pleasured him.

"More," Tristan groaned, a hand reaching up and cupping the back of Wade's head.

He'd always imagined that might make him feel trapped, contained, *pushed*. But instead, he felt worshipped, the same way he was worshipping Tristan. He leaned into it, taking even more in, feeling Tristan's cock hit the back of his throat. He swallowed convulsively, trying not to choke on it.

"That's good, God, that's so good," Tristan moaned above him.

Wade wanted to give him more, wanted to give him everything he ever wanted, but he also needed to breathe, so he backed out a little, giving himself a second. "Sorry," he mumbled around the cock in his mouth.

"It's okay, you can always practice on a banana for next time," Tristan said, his voice a caress. "It's so good, I'm . . ."

Wade didn't let him finish the sentence, just went deep again, sucking hard, and felt every muscle in Tristan's body tense.

He moved a hand in, spreading Tristan's thighs wider, and tugged on his balls, the way he liked his own to be tugged, and it seemed his guy liked that too, because he got even louder.

They were really going to have to figure out a way to keep this under wraps while at camp, and that was going to be tough because Tristan couldn't seem to be quiet.

Wade knew he should be worrying, but there was nothing in his head, just the endless static of giving and receiving pleasure. His own dick was rock hard and aching, desperate to be touched, but when he was making Tristan feel this good, it was surprisingly easy to ignore.

And then above him, Tristan tensed hard, everything trembling, and he choked out a single, "Uh," before his cock jerked and Wade was convulsively swallowing not wanting to lose a single drop.

"Oh my God," Tristan exhaled unsteadily. "You . . . I'm . . ."

Wade gave one last suck, not wanting it to end, not wanting to let go of this moment. But Tristan was shaking like a leaf, overwhelmed, and so he let his cock slip from his mouth and he rocked back on his heels, hands still resting on Tristan's thighs.

It took a moment for Tristan to gather himself, and Wade found himself feeling very smug about this particular fact. He hadn't been sure he'd be good at this, that he'd even enjoy it, but he'd loved every moment of it.

It had been so good when Tristan had sucked him, and he hadn't thought anything could feel any better than that, but giving him that same pleasure . . . it had been overwhelming in the very best kind of way.

"You really didn't have to," Tristan said, finally. "I'm fucking glad you did, obviously, but . . . there's never any pressure." His hand reached down and cupped Wade's cheek, squeezing gently. "Never."

"I wanted to," Wade said simply. "And I loved doing it."

"Well, you can do it any time you want, no arguments from me," Tristan teased. "Now get up here, you're a little too dressed for me."

Wade's fingers were still trembling as he helped Tristan strip off his clothes. And he shook when Tristan closed a hand around his dick. He didn't think he'd ever been so hard in his whole life. But then that was what Tristan did to him. Tristan, and the feelings surging inside him that he'd never felt before, never in his whole life.

"Kiss me," Tristan directed, "and I'm gonna make you feel good."

It was so easy to lean in and let their mouths meet, the kiss both sweet and wild, hot and gentle, as Tristan worked him with his fist, pleasure surging through him.

Tristan was just as much of a tease, and he drew it out, his movements slowing whenever Wade started to get close, and then accelerating once the moment had passed.

When he finally came, it felt like he was exploding from the inside out, the pleasure surging through him like electricity, altering every molecule until there wasn't a single one that Tristan hadn't been imprinted on.

When it ended, they sat there for a long second, both of them panting in the sudden quiet.

"I think . . ." Tristan said thoughtfully, "that we might have to request a room that's apart from everyone."

"I tried to be quiet," Wade said self-consciously. Though at the end, maybe he hadn't tried very hard. It had felt too good to even worry about who might hear.

"Of course you did," Tristan said, gently pushing him to the side so he could get up and clean up.

He came back with a washcloth, and gave Wade a wipe before tossing it into the laundry bin and cuddling back up with him on the bed.

"I just wasn't very successful?" Wade asked, even though he knew the truth.

"I don't think I was very successful, either," Tristan answered ruefully. "Everyone is going to hate us."

"They're going to be jealous of all the fun we're having," Wade said very firmly. The idea of coming out, of being honest with the whole world, still made him break into a bit of a cold sweat, but he was getting better with it.

Now after telling Coach, he thought he even wanted to tell the rest of their teammates.

He wasn't afraid of what they'd say. All he felt was a sense of pride, that he'd won this man over.

This incredible fucking man.

"I'm happy," Tristan said softly, resting his head on Wade's shoulder. "I thought I was happy before, but I think my life was kinda empty. Like one of those big houses that's gorgeous outside, but then you go inside and it doesn't even have furniture."

"I want my house to be lived in," Wade declared softly. "I want a life." He hesitated, but decided that he didn't care anymore about what was right or wrong or if it was too early. "I want a life with you."

"Well, that's handy," Tristan said sleepily. "Because I want a life with you, too. A life and football, and lots of touchdowns. And you. Most of all, you."

"Then, that's exactly what you'll get," Wade said and pulled the blanket over them.

EPILOGUE

TRISTAN WASN'T SO MUCH nervous as he was excited.

"You need to sit down," Wade said, amused as he watched him pace back and forth in the locker room.

"I'm just . . . I'm ready," Tristan said. His helmet was on the bench next to Wade's, but he was already fully dressed in his Piranhas uniform. If Wade's admiring looks were any indication, he looked damn good in the bright turquoise and yellow. But then Wade always thought he looked good, no matter what he wore.

Secretly, Tristan thought Wade liked him best when he wasn't wearing anything at all.

"You sure are," Wade said. "Couldn't be more ready. The last practice, you tore it up."

"Kept Sea Bass on his toes, that's for sure," Tristan said, feeling that surge of excitement rising in him again.

He had never been more ready to play a game of football in his life. He knew just how lucky he was that he'd found a place here, with the Piranhas, with a quarterback like Pax Kelly throwing to him, and guys like Logan and Rob blocking for him. And then there was Wade, playing right next to him.

The man he loved.

Not that he'd told him yet.

He'd been very, very tempted, the day they'd both found out that they'd made the fifty-two-man final roster.

Alec had told him it was going to happen; after his great performance during the preseason games, it had been nearly an inevitability, but he'd still worried. When you found something this good, you didn't want to give it up. You'd fight as hard as it took to keep it.

But just after the meeting with Coach Dawson, right when Wade had hugged him as hard as he'd ever been hugged in his whole damn life, Beau had shown up to congratulate them, and the moment had been broken.

The words had been buzzing under his skin since then.

He thought he wasn't the only one, because there was a way Wade looked at him that couldn't be mistaken for anything else, but then he hadn't said them either.

Tristan thought he'd come the closest the day they'd started to tell their teammates that they were together.

Sebastian had taken one look at them and just thrown his head back and laughed.

"Did you think it was a secret?" he'd asked, clearly very amused. "Really?"

"Well . . . yes," Wade had said carefully. "I . . . we've tried to keep it one, until now."

Sebastian had leaned in and said, very seriously, "Then maybe you should have tried to orgasm a little quieter."

"Seriously," Pax had added in. "I had to buy a better pair of noise-canceling headphones."

Wade had gone bright red. It had been adorable. Tristan had wanted to drag him back to their room and make a whole lot more noise.

"I'm sorry, I just . . . I . . . like . . . Tristan so much."

"We know, man, we really know." Sebastian had patted him on the shoulder. "You two are cute as hell or else we'd have given you hell."

Tristan had wondered if that day he'd meant to say another *L* word, and not *like*, but Wade was surprisingly sweet and sensitive, and of course he wouldn't have wanted to tell Tristan he loved him by telling Sebastian Howard *first*.

He'd been sure it would happen after that, soon after that, but while Wade had continued to be warm and caring and demonstrating in every action that he did love him, he'd never said the words.

Tristan was beginning to think that he was going to have to take one for the team here and be the one to break the stalemate.

"Seriously, come sit down," Wade said again. "You're going to wear yourself out on adrenaline now, before you even get on the field."

"First *real* NFL game, you can't tell me you're not feeling it," Tristan said, coming to stand next to Wade, but not taking a seat.

There was no way he could sit down now. Not when he felt this jittery.

It was the excitement over the game, of course, but it was those words burning just under his skin too.

They were working him up and turning him inside out.

He'd never once been tempted to say them before, and now he could barely stop himself from saying them.

"I'm feeling it," Wade said, grinning. "I'm feeling you."

"Ew, gross," Beau said, coming to a stop in front of them. "Keep it in your pants, dude."

"If it wasn't in my pants, you'd know," Wade said, waggling his eyebrows.

It was a beautiful thing, seeing Wade become freer and freer about his sexuality. It had come in fits and starts at first, but telling Coach Dawson and then the team a week later had started a flood.

Tristan had a feeling that he wouldn't want to keep it under wraps at all soon.

He'd mentioned it to Alec, and Alec had only cautioned him to be sure.

"You mean like . . . pining after your guy for ten years sure?" Tristan had teased him back. He knew just how long Alec and his boyfriend had liked each other, and had done *nothing* about it. Chase Riley had made sure to tell him all about it.

"Yes," Alec had said crisply, and Tristan had heard his eye roll even through the phone.

The thing was, Tristan had never been so sure about anything in his whole goddamned life as he was about Wade.

A close second was playing football for the Piranhas, which was why he was so goddamned worked up.

He couldn't wait to get out there and show the world how hard he'd worked, how much better he'd gotten. How he could truly help his team now.

Lining up on the opposite side of Wade? That was totally the icing on the cake.

"Just wanted to make sure you two are ready," Beau said.

"We're good, if Tristan can stop vibrating on this annoying-as-hell frequency," Wade said. But the way he was smiling let Tristan know that he wasn't actually annoyed at all. He was endeared.

That was just like Wade.

God, he loved him.

"Good," Beau said with an approving nod. "You ready to go kick some ass?"

"Yes," they said together. Looking over at each other, they burst into laughter.

Beau shook his head. "Sebastian is right. I never know whether to think you're cute or to knock your heads together."

"Former," Tristan said, at the same time as Wade said, "Latter."

Beau walked off, shaking his head.

"You really okay?" Wade asked again. "You haven't stopped pacing."

Tristan glanced around. The other players were sitting around or milling around in smaller groups, mostly minding their own business, getting prepped for the upcoming battle.

He and Wade had agreed to leave any physical PDA out of the locker room. It wasn't the place for it. The locker room was the place where they focused on football. But how could Tristan focus when this *huge* thing was unsaid between them? And he'd promised Coach that he wouldn't let the relationship distract from football.

"I . . . you know you're part of the reason I'm here at all," Tristan said.

"That is bullshit," Wade scoffed. "You're here because you've got incredible natural skill and you've worked your ass off to hone it."

"Yeah," Tristan said uncertainly. He'd never said this before, and it turned out it was hard to just blurt it out, especially when Wade was *Wade*, and wouldn't fucking take a compliment.

"You helped me *want* it, though," Tristan said forging ahead. "I . . . you know how much I care about you, right? I . . . I . . ." He hesitated, hating himself for the sudden frisson of fear. He knew the way Wade looked at him. It was love. There was no way around it. Then why was it so hard to say?

Wade's face softened, the look in his pale gray eyes almost unbearable, it was so sweet and caring. "I love you, too," he said quietly.

At first it didn't even register what he'd said.

Then it did, and Tristan just stared at him.

"Did you . . ."

"I did," Wade said with a nod. "Because you seemed to be having some trouble. Thought I'd help you out." He smiled. "Do you love me, too? I kinda thought you might."

"I do, I do love you," Tristan said, the words tumbling out of him. And despite their very firm agreement on no PDA in the locker room, bent down and hugged the crap out of his boyfriend, pads and all. "I love you so goddamned much."

When Tristan pulled away, he was smiling so bright that Tristan felt like his heart must have expanded a few sizes. He offered a hand to his boyfriend. To the man he fucking *loved*.

His lover.

His teammate.

His forever.

"Come on, sweetcheeks," he said, "let's go play some football."

Catch up with Sebastian and Beau, and the rest of the Miami Piranhas in *Playing for Keeps*, book one of this exciting football series from Beth Bolden.

INTERESTED IN READING MORE OF
BETH'S BOOKS?

CHECK OUT A FULL LIST OF TILES
BY SCANNING THE QR CODE
OR VISITING HER WEBSITE

WWW.BETHBOLDEN.COM/BOOKLIST

WANT TO FOLLOW BETH?

MAKE SURE YOU NEVER
MISS A RELEASE?

SCAN THE QR CODE BELOW
OR VISIT HER WEBSITE
FOR A SOCIAL MEDIA LIST,
NEWSLETTER SIGNUP,
AND SO MUCH MORE!

WWW.BETHBOLDEN.COM/ABOUT